You Can Call Me

LIZZIE,

A Series of Short Adventures

JK Hoffman

ISBN 978-1-954345-39-3 (paperback)
ISBN 978-1-954345-40-9 (hardcover)
ISBN 978-1-954345-41-6 (digital)

Rushmore Press LLC
1 800 460 9188
www.rushmorepress.com

Printed in the United States of America

This book is dedicated to Fourth and Fifth Generations Nieces and Nephews of Lizzie Hoffman

Fourth Generation:

Riley Fallaha   Aiden Fallaha

Devon Kuczyinski   Ciarra Kuczyinski

Alexa Hoffman   Maceo Hare

Thomas Hoffman   Jonathan Hoffman

James Eckstenkemper   Ashley Eckstenkemper
Cody Eckstenkemper

Caleb Hoffman   Evan Hoffman
Dana Hoffman

Tikanna Hoffman   William Hoffman
Faith Hoffman

Fifth Generation:

Aura Eckstenkemper   Ezquial Michael Hoffman

LIVE YOUR LIFE LIZZIE STRONG!

Contents

PART THREE

Authors Thoughts

Welcome to the wonderful life of Lizzie.

In my first book, *'Flagstaff's Forgotten Cowgirl,' {Now known as Forgotten Cowgirl}*, I wrote about Lizzie's incredible life in the later part of the 19th century to the early 20th century. We followed her from the high deserts on a ranch in New Mexico to the frigid winters of the Yukon and back to her home in the mountain town of Flagstaff, Arizona. In writing this amazing woman's life I became connected to her. Long after the book was published, my mind would not stop making up stories about her. I was hooked.

I wrote this book as a series of short adventures. My goal was that I wanted to write a book that would appeal to all ages. Hoping that a young or old person, who is feeling lonely, will find out what it is like to make a friend in a book. I did. Mine was *Nancy Drew.* Who was yours?

Imagine a day when you want to hang out with friends. You call people and invite them to come out. No one can do anything. You find yourself alone, you are starting to feel sorry for yourself. Suddenly, the corner of this book catches your eye. Aha! Read the book.

In a few moments, you find yourself running, and riding with Lizzie. You are not lonely. You just made a new friend. She is yours to use your imagination. A book is a great friend that will be waiting for you.

As I have said before,

If you find yourself getting goosebumps or a shiver up your spine when you think or talk about her out of nowhere, then you can say that you

"Have you been bitten by the Lizzie bug?"

Welcome aboard; all are welcome. Give me a review, tell your friends. Most of all, enjoy the book.

LIZZIE HOFFMAN~1876 to 1911
The picture is Property of JK Hoffman

HOW I CAME TO BE ME

My name is Elisabeth Mae Hoffman, but you can call me Lizzie. I wouldn't fit the name Elisabeth, even if it was my grandmother's name. Don't get me wrong; fit is a perfectly good name, but not for me. Let me rephrase that last sentence; it does not suit me. I am Lizzie.

My oldest brother George (he is nearing thirty), likes to tease me and say, "Busy, Lizzie. She is always having tizzies." Then I get mad and bang on his back as hard as I can. He tells me to hit him here and there. Apparently, he has a sore back, and it feels good to him. I laugh, and he tickles me; I tickle him back.

He used to call my older sister, "Smelly, Nellie. You smell like jelly." My other sister Tillie is, "Tillie is all frilly and silly." He never calls you by your real name unless you are in trouble with him. Which is practically never because George is a good man. My other two brothers are never around much. As you can see, there are six of us children in the family.

I am a genuine tomboy; inside and out. Why I would rather be outside from sun-up to sun-down every day. Indoor makes me feel as if I am trapped like a caged animal or something. I remember a time when my sisters had to hold me down so that mama could fit a dress to me. I even got stuck with one of the sewing pins and did not cry.

Mama knows how to punish me; she just makes me stay inside and do housework and sewing chores. Ironing…now there is one chore I thoroughly despise. She hands me a whole pile of hankies to press. Now, why on earth does a person need a neatly ironed piece of cloth to blow one's nose on?

Give me a chore outside, and I will be as happy as a dog with a bone. My brothers like it. They will give me the chores that they don't like doing, and sometimes I can even get them to buy me a soda or candy when we are in town.

Daddy seems to be the only one who can see right through me. He tells me that because I am the youngest out of the bunch, I have to be spoiled a little. Mama chews him out if she hears him tell me that. Daddy and I have an understanding. He gives me a wink, and I give him one back. It is like having a secret with someone.

I came in on a cyclone, or so my daddy always told me. I was born on the Fourth of September in Union Center, Kansas. My family had just moved to Kansas by way of a wagon train from Michigan. Daddy got word that they were homesteading land for people who were willing to work the area. He had a hard time swaying my mama that she should leave her home and family and travel in a wagon out to the prairie. It took quite a bit of convincing since mama had just given birth to her fifth child, my sister Tillie. There were seven people in my family, ranging in age from one to forty-three. Of course, after I came along, which made eight. Nellie became mama's helper. Two children under five on a farm was challenging. However, Nellie was a natural-born mother.

It was nearing time for mama to give birth to me. Johnny was at an age when he did not, and you could not explain to him about giving birth. He thought mama was going to die. He cried and cried at the thought, and no amount of explanation would calm him down. Her contractions began. She tried not to scare him with her moans. Everyone was busy, and he had seemed to settle down.

George left on horseback to get the neighbor lady to help with my birth. As he was riding, he saw the funnel cloud headed right towards us. He decided to turn around and head back home.

When he returned without the neighbor, daddy was beside himself. Every other birth, mama had a midwife to help her. Never had he delivered a baby. Mama tried to explain to him that it was no different from helping a cow or horse give birth, and he had done that many times. She tried to reassure him that everyone would be fine.

It was during that commotion that Johnny must have gotten scared and ran outside without anyone noticing he was gone.

Suddenly, daddy said in a very concerned voice, "Where is Johnny?"

George and Nellie offered to find him. He was nowhere to be found.

Nellie looked up at the ominous clouds moving fast through the sky. It became gloomy, and the wind started to blow.

Nellie rushed to the house and came inside, yelling, "Cyclone. It is here already."

They had to get mama down into the cellar and fast. George was the last one down. No Johnny. Everyone knew they could not tell mama a word about Johnny. She would be too upset.

The door was only closed at the very last minute. Daddy said that was the hardest decision he ever had to make.

The wind could be heard overhead. Lightning and thunder popped all around.

Someone said as I was being born, that I came in with a cyclone. Mama said it felt like a twister when I was coming out.

The noise above the cellar calmed. No one knew how long we had been down there. Daddy cautiously pushed the doors of the cellar open. George and Bertie had to help him. Luckily, Bertie was small enough he could climb through the debris covering the top and clear it sufficiently to get them open.

The glare of sunlight practically blinded everyone because they had been in the dark with only a couple of candles for so long.

Mama and I slept while everyone else was frantically looking for Johnny.

Miraculously, after searching everywhere, they found Johnny lying face down in a ditch daddy had dug earlier in the week.

It was days later when mama heard the story. She exclaimed, "Thank the Lord that everyone was safe."

Johnny did not want to call me cyclone, and the family agreed that they would not call me that again.

I think the stories of my birth later gave me momentum to live my life like the way I came into this world, a cyclone.

My hair was as black as night, with an abundance of it. Mama said that I reminded her of a doll she admired in a store window in Baden, Germany. You see, my parents, Adam and Mary Josephine, were immigrants from Germany. Mama came with her family when she was about eighteen years old. Daddy came by himself and was a shoe cobbler apprentice. Daddy worked with leather and made shoes.

Mama and daddy met when mama was a housekeeper for a family in Monroe, Michigan. She would take shoes to daddy's shop for repair. Mama knew that he was the one for her. Then one day, she took shoes in for repair, and he was not there. When asked where he was, they told her that he went back to Germany. She was distressed. How could he leave without telling her? Is he coming back? No one knew. She left the shop feeling broken-hearted.

Sometime later, she returned to the shop. To her surprise, the man told her that he had something for her. She waited anxiously for the man to return. To her amazement, he had a letter to her from Adam. She could barely contain her excitement but chose to wait to read it when she arrived home.

Adam told her that he had finished his apprenticeship and had decided to return to Germany. However, things at home were not as he had remembered. Being gone made him realize that his life was better in America. It would take time, but he would return to Michigan. He also told her of his intent to ask her to marry him.

Upon reading those words, Mary let out a gasp. He felt the same way she did. She would wait for him for as long as it took him. Hurriedly, she immediately penned a letter back to him. They continued writing to each other until he returned.

Soon after he got back, they married in a beautiful church in Grand Rapids, Michigan. It was a small intimate ceremony. Attended only by two witnesses.

Adam immediately set to work as a shoe cobbler. He was skilled in leather and could make hats and belts, shoes, and saddles, etc.

I love that story, don't you? It gives me goose pimples every time I tell that story.

Mama, having lost her mother at a young age, was thrilled to have a family. Her grandmother raised her until she was fourteen. She remembered the day very vividly when her father appeared and took her away from the beautiful green valley she loved. Life became difficult with her new family. Then one day, her father announced that they were moving to America.

Mary was heartbroken. Her grandmother was like her mother. She was leaving everything that she was familiar with and loved.

Her father remarried, and she had several half-brothers and sisters. Ironically, a similar event happened to Adam.

A year later, my oldest brother George was born. Life, as Mama used to say, was simple. The three of them were happy living a quiet existence.

Then the big war between the States began. They were Northerners and the men were joining forces with the Union. The fight against slavery began.

Adam was a proud American. He joined the army and was going off to serve his country.

Mary was left behind with George. They moved to Monroe to be close to family. George loved the attention and being the man of the house. He matured quickly out of necessity. George had promised his father that he would take care of his mother while daddy was away. George was a quiet, serious boy. He loved growing up in Monroe.

Daddy was positioned as a saddlery man. He made saddles and reins and any other leather goods the army needed. When he returned home from the war, his leg had been injured.

They then had two more children, Nellie and Bertie. Life grew more difficult and harder to support a family. He would hear the men talking about the land to the west. There was fertile farmland in Kansas. Talking with his wife, she was not in favor of moving a family of young children across the Plains, especially after Johnny was born. It would be a challenge.

After a series of hardships and the birth of Tillie, mama gave in to daddy's insistence. She agreed to leave Michigan and travel by covered wagon west. As luck, for me, would have it, mama was pregnant. I was the only one not born in Michigan.

The family of seven loaded the household belongings and moved west. I have heard that it took about three months with every kind of weather imaginable. The trip was hard on mama.

They arrived in time to get in a small crop on the homestead. A homestead is a piece of land given to you by the government. You have to promise to build a house on it and farm. If you did not, after five years, the government would take it back. If you did as they asked, the land became yours to keep.

So, life began for the family of eight in South-East, Kansas.

Picture of Tillie and Nellie in Albuquerque,
New Mexico early 1880s

PART ONE

UNION CENTRE, KANSAS TO
NEW MEXICO~1876–1882
AGES~0–10

FABRIC FLOUR SACK WHICH CAN BE USED
IN MAKING DOLLS SUCH AS SASS-A-FRASS

CHAPTER 1

Sass-A-Frass

Union Centre, Kansas~1879
Age~3

On my third birthday, I received a special present. I was given a doll, not just any doll. It was my doll. She belonged to me. Not Nellie or Tillie, not a hand-me-down doll. All mine. Mama said so. Her hair was as dark as mine, not the usual red-headed dolls everyone else had. Not the ragged doll-like so many girls got. She was beautiful. She wore a red checkered dress with a white pinafore and a red bow in her hair.

Mama says that a lady she knows made it special for me. She was the best present that I had ever received.

I went to bed that night, not having to fight Tillie for her doll. I had my own. We laid in my half of the feather bed, and I began telling her secrets. Not that a three-year-old has many secrets, but what I told her was the most important idea I could make up.

She was the most adorable doll I had ever seen. Her black eyes [like mine] were stitched on her face. Her dress could come off.

"Sass-A-Frass, you are wearing a petticoat. Tillie's doll doesn't have one on. You are special. Oh, look," I say as I undress her, "I see something. Did somebody mark on you? I wish I could read. Mama, mama, come here."

Mama came in very concerned. "Did you have a nightmare?"

"No, mama, look, look at my doll. Somebody marked on her. Who did that?"

"Let me see, dear," bringing the candle closer. I heard mama giggle and say, "It is writing on the cloth. The doll is made from a flour sack as I have in the kitchen. She is stuffed inside with straw. It is how she is made. Now get to sleep. You can look at her more closely tomorrow."

The day after your birthday is kind of a letdown. All week, the whole family paid attention to me. "Who's having a birthday?" or "I get to spank you on your birthday." Then the next day, no one says anything to you.

I don't remember much about being three. Only having a big dislike for grasshoppers. My brothers would put them down my back, and I would run off screaming to mama or Nellie.

Nellie was my biggest sister. At thirteen, and being the oldest girl, she played mother to my youngest brother Johnny, Tillie, and me. Believe me, with her voice; she could get anyone to listen. She had the voice of a schoolmarm. Everyone stood up and took notice. She was just a born leader. Anyhow, that is what mama always said.

As mama explained, she could not raise six kids and run a farm alone. Nellie was her helper. It was just her personality, who she is, and the oldest girl, so naturally, it would seem that she was her favorite child.

I took my doll to my mama Nellie. I had completely undressed her and, I could not get the clothes back on her, and I needed help with the two buttons.

"Why did you take her clothes off? Silly girl."

"I wanted to see flour writing."

"The flour writing? Do you mean the flour sack? Oh look, here on her chest is a heart with your name Lizzie sewed in the fabric."

"Where? Let me see. Oh, I like that."

"You don't like the flour sack writing, though?"

"No, make it go away. I don't like it."

"You just have to keep her clothes on, and no one will see the marks. You have heard daddy talk about everyone's distinguishing characteristic, haven't you?"

"Yes, he says everyone has one, and you should be proud of it. It makes you special, like a birthmark. I have one. Is this Sassy's birthmark?"

"Yes, exactly. Now, let's get this baby dressed."

"Thank you, mama Nellie."

Sass-a-frass, or Sassy as I began calling her, was always with me. She went wherever I went. The ladies at church would comment on what a fine doll I had. Mama introduced me to the lady who made her. She told me that she thought Sassy was the most beautiful doll she had ever made. I agreed with her.

Fall was well upon us. I had to go out in the fields with everyone to pick the crop.

I was with the boys in the cornfield, on the wagon, mind you. My job was to help throw the ears of corn to the front of the wagon. We worked out all day long.

"Johnny, I am tired."

"Okay, sister, just a minute, and I will carry you down, and you can lie underneath the wagon in the shade."

"Don't forget about Sassy. She needs a nap."

"Okay, I won't."

I must have fallen right to sleep because the next thing I knew was that mama was tucking me in my bed. I was so tired that I did not even eat supper.

"Mama, mama, where is she?' I was screaming at the top of my lungs.

Mama rushed in and said, "Where is who?"

"Sassy, where is my Sassy doll?"

"I am sure she is fine. We will find, her I promise. Get dressed and come down and eat before we head back out to the field."

I ate my porridge as fast as I could and went out of the door. Frantically, I searched. I went over to the wagon, where the boys were unloading the ears of corn.

"Have you seen Sassy? I can't find her."

Johnny said from inside the wagon, "She's not up here where you had her?"

George said, "I picked her up along with you yesterday."

"You had her in your hand when I carried you inside," yelled Bertie.

"Can you help me find her? I need her."

All three yelled, "Yes, as soon as we finish up here."

I moped back to the house. Tillie was with Nellie in the chicken coop.

"Why are you so somber today, child?"

"It's Sassy; I can't find her."

Tillie named off places to see if I had looked everywhere; my bed, the floor, the wagon.

"Yes, I have looked everywhere."

"When we get done here, we will help you look."

Everyone, including daddy, searched through the house for her. Still no Sassy.

Finally, daddy said, "Time to get going. We will probably find her in the field."

We loaded up the supplies and food for the day and daddy drove the wagon out to our last stop the day before.

To my great disappointment, there was no Sassy to be found. Everyone, it seemed, told me to put it aside for now. We have work to do, and we will look later.

I worked as hard as I could. Bertie told me that you could put your worries aside the harder you work. I tried. I still could not help but think about her.

Today, I did not fall asleep. I wanted to be awake and look when we got back to the house.

Daddy was complaining about his leg today, an injury from the war. We stopped picking earlier in the day.

When we arrived back at the house, the dogs were excited to be home. They were playing with each other and running back and forth, acting a little more rambunctious than normal.

Johnny went over by them. They had something they were playing with. They were tossing it into the air and biting it with their teeth, tugging on it as hard as they could jerk.

There in the dirt, was the remnant of straw and cloth strewn about. Black yarn lay in a twisted mess with straw and dirt tangled within the braids. There in the dirt lay the heart with Lizzie on it.

Johnny knew that I would be crushed. He carefully picked up the tattered bits and pieces of what was left of Sassy.

I was in the house when he came in and whispered to mama, asking her for some wrapping paper.

She asked him why, and he showed her something in his hand.

"Oh, oh, dear, oh my. How?" Mama tried to ask him without letting on to me as to what he had found.

She got up from her sewing and handed him a leftover piece of paper from the mercantile. She always neatly folded the wrapping paper to reuse.

Mama looked at Johnny questioningly, and he seemed to know what she meant.

"It is okay, Mama; I will take care of this for now. You girls can do the rest. I am a scaredy-cat when it comes to things like that."

After supper, everyone gathered around, and mama began telling me about Sassy. She handed me the remains of Sassy wrapped neatly inside the brown paper. I wailed and cried and probably screamed a bit. They all let me throw my tantrum until I cried myself to sleep.

The next day, I solemnly announced at breakfast that there would be a funeral later in the day for Sass-A-Frass.

All agreed that would be fitting, and everyone helped out digging her a small grave under the elm tree.

It was a short service. We had all changed into our Sunday best, and daddy said a prayer for her to go to doll heaven.

I kept the heart with my name on it neatly tucked inside a little box with my treasures.

Tillie shared her doll with me, but it was not the same. A piece of my heart was chewed up and spat out with the dog's playfulness.

George said that he once had a dog that liked to chew up everything in sight.

I would go and sit under the tree at times and talk to her. I know she was listening. That helped me feel better.

Christmas came with lots of snow. We had been snowed in for days just before the big day.

Our packages were few under a little tree decorated with popcorn strings. I placed the little heart on the tree.

Mama was cooking dinner when there was a knock at the door. We all ran to see who could possibly be visiting.

It was a man driving his sleigh.

"Ho, Ho, Ho!" he said. I have a special delivery from Santa Clause for a Miss Lizzie Hoffman."

Everyone cleared the way for me, and the man brought a package out from behind his back and said, "Merry Christmas!"

I was shaking as I took the package and held it.

"Go ahead, Lizzie, open it." Everyone agreed and seemed delighted that I should be the only one receiving a package.

There, wrapped neatly in special Christmas paper and tied with the biggest bow I had ever seen, lay Sassy. I was her, all fixed up and clean with fresh straw stuffed inside her.

I hugged the man and looked up to see that he had a tear running down his cheek. Then I looked at everyone else and saw them crying.

It was the best Christmas ever for Sassy and me.

Sassy,

I said to her that night in bed, "I am so glad to have you back home with me."

How did you get out from under the elm tree? You will never tell me, but I bet all of them downstairs knows. It was them. Even so, you and I will keep a secret that I figured it out."

You know that you are loved when those around you know your special things.

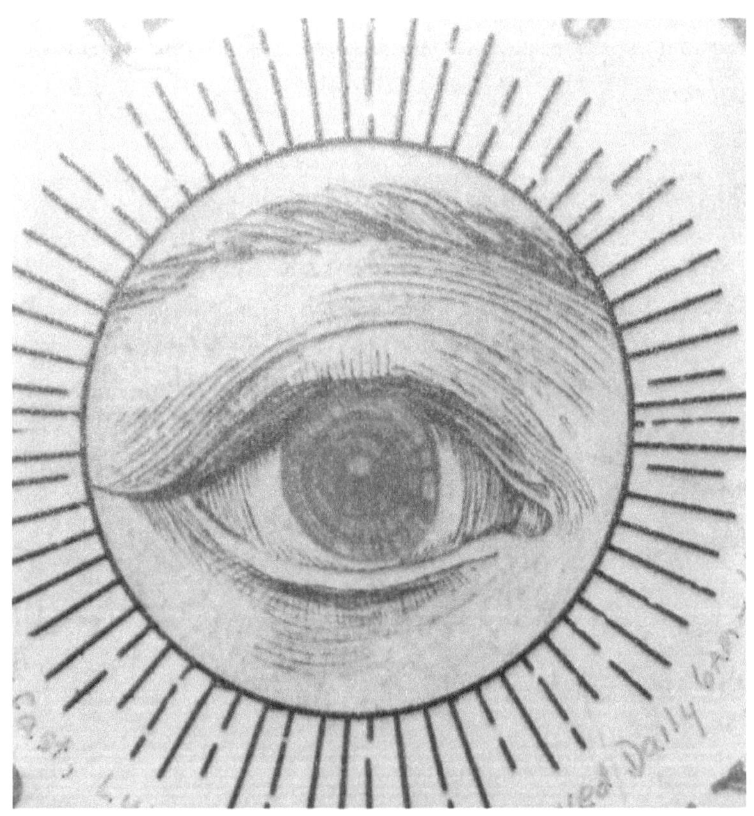

The seeing eye is watching you. It sees all.
The picture is property of JK Hoffman

CHAPTER 2

The Peddler and the Fortune Teller

Union Centre, Kansas~1880
Age~4

Tillie and I walked to town. She was in a hurry to get the errands completed for mama. This was mama's mending day, and she needed buttons and thread. I was in no hurry to return to the house.

"Hurry up, Lizzie. I know I should have left you at home. You promised me that you would stay up with me."

"I am hot and tired, Tillie. I can't walk any faster."

"I should take you back home right now."

Out on the Kansas plains, the sun beat down, and the hot gusts blew around us. The wind was not offering any relief to our warm bodies. There was nothing to stop the wind. It pushed against us, trying to hold us back.

"Turn around, Tillie, and walk backward. Look, the dirt doesn't get into my eyes."

"It's too slow."

"I can run backward, can you?"

Tillie tried, but her skirt was longer than mine, and her feet got twisted in the skirt. She fell into me, and we both went down in the dirt.

"Now look at us; we are filthy. We look like ragamuffins. Even my hair is falling down," she complained.

We brushed ourselves off and trudged on.

I could see a wagon up ahead. As we approached, we walked up to it slowly.

Mama's words were echoing in my head. "Stay away from strangers. Be polite, but don't dally."

It was a peddler's wagon. I have never seen one this close before. The wood on the wagon's sides was old and weather-worn. Pieces of wood were missing from the frame. There were shovels, picks, along with cast-iron pots and skillets tied to the outside of the wagon. Horse tethers and reins. Just to mention a few of the items I saw from the side.

My curiosity was aroused. I wanted to stop and look inside. It was so fun to see a store on wheels.

Tillie gave me a look. I knew from her face that I was supposed to hasten my walk.

I couldn't see anyone around the wagon. Odd. A peddler does not leave his belongings unattended.

An old dog barked from inside the wagon as we walked. That dog would not scare off a soul. He was skinny, and matted gray hair covered his body. The dog had what looked like a scruffy beard. He had drool coming from his mouth.

"Don't look into a dog's eyes." Tillie scolded.

"I didn't."

"You did too; I saw you."

So much for being quiet. Neither of us admitted to arguing, and neither one of us was giving in.

We kept walking, leaving the wagon behind us.

Our first stop in town was at the Post Office. Mama wrote letters to family. She did not do it often, but when she did write, the letters were usually long.

The postman had a candy stick for both of us.

"Thank you, mister." We both said in unison.

"You girls take this mail to your mama. I have been holding on to it for at least a fortnight now. It would have gone into the unclaimed pile pretty soon. Except, I know your mama and daddy. I know your family has a difficult time getting into town. Is your daddy's leg still giving him fits?"

"Yes, sir," answered Tillie.

"The men our age suffers from one thing or another cause of that darned war. It didn't get us while we were fighting, but it still haunts us with pain and suffering. Tell them I said, "Hello.""

"Yes, sir, we sure will. Thanks again for the candy."

"Will we get candy every place we go today?"

"Yes, Bertie says that old people like to give children candy. It is their way of spoiling us. Most all the children here in Kansas left their old people behind because the trip was too hard. Because we don't have grandparents, they all fill in for them."

"I want my grandparents."

"You will have to make do with other folks. None of ours is left."

We went to the general store next. We picked up thread and buttons. Then as we were leaving, we got to pick out a stick of candy. I put this one in my pocket to save for later. Peppermint, my favorite. The peppermint filled my head as I sucked on the stick of sweet candy.

We stopped at the water pump to wash the sticky off our hands. I stuck my head under it and asked Tillie to pump. The cold water felt good as it ran over my head.

A loud voice saying, "What are you two girls doing over there? No vagrants and no loitering. Get on your way now."

My wet hair was down in front of my face, and apparently, the dirt from earlier was smeared on my face. Tillie looked about the same. As we looked at each other over, we could understand why the sheriff did not recognize us immediately.

"Sheriff, we are not vagrants; we are Hoffman's from Union Centre."

"What on earth happened to you? Are you in town alone?"

"Yes, sir."

"You two girls hungry? I was just going over to the cafe to get lunch." He handed us his hanky to wipe our faces.

"We have no extra money for lunch, sir," Tillie said immediately.

"I am hungry, Tillie."

"What is your name, little one?

"Cyclone Lizzie I was brought in on a cyclone."

"You were not, Lizzie. That is a fable."

"No, sir. Mama and daddy tell me so."

The sheriff laughed as he motioned for us to follow him to the cafe. He told us that since girls didn't eat more than a baby bird, he could afford to buy us lunch.

I had to think about that one for a while. Birds eat worms. Yuck.

The sheriff walked in with us in tow.

"Give us three of today's specials, Molly. With three big glasses of milk."

We sat at a long counter beside other men. I could barely see over the wood plank. Tillie told me to sit on my feet.

They served us ham with greens and potatoes. It tasted good for a stranger's cooking. It is pretty good. Mama always said she only liked her own cooking. I think this lady is a pretty good cook. When she came out of the kitchen, I noticed her beautiful smile, and her skin was dark. She was the most attractive woman I had ever seen.

I spoke up and told her that the food was good.

Her voice was an accent I had never before heard.

"If you like that, try this spice on your food." She handed us a little bottle of sauce. "Just do not use too much."

Both of us added a small drop on the greens and tasted it; we could not breathe for a bit. It was hotter than anything we had ever tried.

Everyone laughed while we tried to catch our breath.

She told us that she was Cajun from Louisiana.

"I like the way you talk," I told her.

"I see something in you. Let me see your palm, child." I eagerly handed it to her. She studied it for some time.

"This can't be," she mumbled to herself.

"What can you see?" asked Tillie anxiously.

"Nothing," she said, dropping my hand. "I should know not to read the children's palms. If you were older, maybe, then I could read it right. Live your life strong."

We were distracted when a man entered the restaurant begging for food. He was a very thin man with a sparse beard. He carried a variety of small things tied to a rope. There were pots and cooking utensils. I even saw tools for woodworking. I was amazed looking at everything. It must be the peddler.

The lady talked him into trading a couple of pots for a meal. He ate the food down so fast; I don't think he had time to taste its goodness.

As we were about to leave, Nellie came in the door looking for us. We got a scolding in front of everyone. She rushed us out of the cafe. As I was walking out of the cafe, I spotted a sign hidden from view of most adults that had a picture of an eye looking out a hole.

"Nellie, can you read that sign to me?"

"It says, LOVE, FATE, DESTINY. I CAN SEE ALL, AND I KNOW ALL." Come on now. We cannot waste a moment; mama is so worried about you two. You should have been back home by now." She held us by our coats and dragged us down the street.

"The sheriff wanted to feed us," I explained. "It would have been rude to say no."

"How did you pay for your food? See that old man over there? He is skin and bones; I bet he hasn't eaten for days." She was pointing at the peddler.

"Yes, he has. He traded his things for food."

"Can we race home?"

"Yes, I will beat you both." Off we took down the dirt road towards home.

As we were running, we passed the peddler's wagon. The old dog barked and howled a pitiful song. I had stuck a roll into my pocket, and I threw it up to him. He quickly went after it.

Long after we were home, I could not stop thinking about the old man. That night at supper, I stashed my bread and some raw carrots into my pinafore. I took the napkin to tie up the food.

At breakfast, I only ate one flapjack. I pretended to be hungry, so mama would give me more and not notice that I was putting them into a napkin. Bertie saw me and cornered me.

"You got some critter you're feeding? Spill the beans or Sassy is mine, and I tell the folks."

"Can you keep a secret?"

"Depends, I guess. What's in it for me?"

"Nothing, cause there is nothing in it for me."

"Nothin? Okay."

"You saw the peddler with the broken-down wagon?"

"Yep."

"He and the dogs are skin and bones. They don't have anything to eat. His wagon is broken down."

"So, you are going to share your food with him? Did you ask mama, if you could?"

"No, she might say no."

"The folks aren't one to let a man starve."

"Would you help me talk to them?"

"Let's go while pop is inside."

Bertie took over and explained to them what I was trying to do.

Soon the whole family was discussing the peddler. George said he had watched him for days. "Harmless, both he and his dog."

"Let's go, boys. Maybe we can fix up his wagon, and the girls can feed him. At least enough to get him on his way."

Daddy and the boys hooked up the wagon, while mama and us girls made up a bundle of food. I made sure there were a couple of carrots for his old mule.

When we pulled up beside him, he was looking pretty down on his luck.

Daddy told him we were there to help. After surveying the damage on the wagon, he said, "Boys, it is, just as I suspected. This wagon is in bad need of repair. Do you mind, sir, if we give you a hand repairing this?"

"I can't pay you. But I can help around your farm. I am a strong, hard worker," he said as he ate the food. "God Bless you."

That night at dinner, we prayed for the peddler and thanked God for our food that we may share."

He stayed around until the wagon was repaired and then headed on his way.

Now Sassy,

It feels good to help someone in need. I was thinking about the Cajun lady in town. Did she see something she didn't want me to know? For some reason, I think that she felt something bad. I will take in those who need a good meal and a place to sleep.

Kindness is the easiest thing you can do in life. If nothing else, a smile will do.

GRASSHOPPER
PICTURE IS PROPERTY OF JK HOFFMAN

CHAPTER 3

Grasshoppers Chase us West

Union Centre, Kansas~1882
Age~5

Daddy and the boys had just gotten the crops in the ground. They worked in the fields from sun-up to sun-down. It was a big relief for everyone when they were done.

That Sunday after church, the whole community celebrated the end of the planting season. Farmers have three important seasons: planting, growing, and harvesting. We were celebrating getting the crop in and praying for a good year on the farm. Everyone was in a festive mood.

The smaller children, including me, huddled together to play. We were focused on a green grasshopper. At age five, there is a fascination for these long-legged creatures.

Another cicada, as they are sometimes called, was found jumping in some tall grass. One of the boys in the group found the green critter and caught it in his hand. We were all amazed at this boy's talent.

We would put them to a race. As it turned out, one was green and the other brown. The girls chose green. Color does matter. Brown was plain and was harder to see.

We placed them side by side, coaxing them to jump down the path someone had made by dragging their shoe on the ground.

We counted; one, two, three, go.

They were off. Not by way of the path. The critters were picked up so many times and moved. Oh no, a leg came off of ours. Then it jumped. Not as good as the boys. Then they had a leg come off. There was no winner because neither could no longer move.

When one of the parents came to check on us, he did not care that we were playing with the locust, as he called the things. Rather, he was concerned that they were there already, so early in the spring.

Quickly, the men gathered to discuss this imposing problem. Locust, grasshoppers, cicada, or any other name spell's trouble for a farmer. Why would grown men care so much about a few grasshoppers? We were about to find out.

Daddy could talk of nothing else as we traveled home in the wagon. He and the boys were planning their attack. Kill as many as possible.

I could not grasp the concept of how two little bugs could cause such a commotion. They are not very big. How could they possibly eat enough to destroy all of our crops?

We did as we were told. We attacked the grasshoppers with full force.

As the days and weeks went on, our crops sprouted. I was sent out with Nellie to survey the northeast corner of our land. We could not walk without disturbing the hordes of them in the grasses. I stepped into one area, and suddenly, they were all over me. I screamed.

Nellie reacted with a scream. We turned around and ran back to the barn.

We gave our report; lots of grasshoppers. Daddy told us to march back out there and see how the plants were doing.

Reluctantly, we went back. This time we took a long stick with us to try to clear the area ahead of us as we were walking. We soon learned that our idea was not working.

There was a fair number of crops growing. Nellie felt as if we were okay for now.

The problem kept worsening with each passing week. A good rainstorm might slow the locust down. No rain in sight.

We had a visitor from another farm up the road, a concerned farmer. They were all perplexed. The two of them decided to have a meeting in town to discuss possible options.

Mama and daddy went to town for the big meeting. We watched the procession of buggies loaded with frustrated farmers making their way to town.

A year without crops to sell would ruin all of us. Could this be a repeat of the great locust invasion of 1874? Two years before we came to this area of Kansas, the locust was the most destructive. Stories were told that the sky in the daytime was dark because of the large quantities of bugs. Anything you owned was eaten by them. Nothing was safe. They hung on your houses, animals, and even people. Before bed, you would have to check the bed for the awful things. As food became scarce, people began eating them. Panic set in, forcing people to leave their homes and go west.

While mama and daddy were gone to town, a swarm of locusts attacked the crops. The boys discovered that there was nothing left but shafts of corn and wheat standing in the field.

I could hear the boys talking among themselves. They were complaining that daddy should have planted the winter hay. No locust in the winter.

George explained that the price of seeds was beyond our daddy's pocketbook. He had done alright in the past. Surely this year would be the same. One good year would change everything.

"We have to take matters into our own hands, boys," said Bertie.

"What are you thinking, Bertie?"

"Fire, like they did back in 1874. Burn the fields. It is the only way to save next year's crops. This year is a total loss. Daddy won't do it himself."

"You mean to burn it now while he is away?" asked George.

"We try just an acre. Not the whole farm. Just to show him what it does."

"Let's take a vote. We are all in this together."

The boys decided to include us, women, in on the vote. Nellie pulled the two of us off to the side and told us to vote no. We should wait until mama and daddy return and let him decide.

We all agreed that the vote would stay, even if we did not like the outcome.

We voted; four to two against setting the field on fire. Done. We would wait for daddy.

No one noticed that Johnny and Bertie were not around shortly after the vote was taken. They agreed to wait.

A storm was blowing in. The wind increased. No rain, just wind.

George smelled the smoke first. He went outside and saw the field on fire. He panicked when he saw the two of them out watching the flames shoot high in the dark sky. "Too close to the house," he yelled. He ran to the cistern to get water.

He tried to water down on the ground near the house. The wind and fire were now our biggest enemies.

Everyone was in town at the meeting. Help was limited to young men the age of our boys.

We gathered our belongings and loaded what we could into the wagon. We also helped water down the house. No use worrying about the fields now. Protect the house and animals in the barn. We had to let the horses, cows, and chickens loose. It was all chaos.

Someone shouted that the roof on the house was on fire. All attention went into the house. Without a house on our land, our homestead would not be finalized. In the contract, it stated that you must have a house. We were only months away from the land, becoming ours. We were ruined.

The winds stopped, and the rain came. Too late to save the farm and the house.

We all sat huddled in the wagon in silence. Johnny and Bertie, quietly awaiting the wrath of daddy. What would daddy do to them?

Daddy appeared as if from nowhere. He lifted the canvas wagon cover and announced that he wanted to speak to whoever was the reason for this disaster.

We all sat quietly together when George and Nellie announced that it was all of us. We took a vote, they told him. We were all responsible for the fire. All eyes turned towards Tillie and me. A look from Nellie told us that we had better agree or that life as we had known it would be over.

"Is that true? You all set the field on fire."

"Yes, sir. You should have seen all the locust. It was as dark as night, with all of them swarming, devouring the crops faster than we could kill them. It was the only way we could think of to save the farm for next year. We saved what we could of the house. "Explained Nellie.

"You did what I was going to come home and do. We had no other options. You have witnessed their destruction, and it was not even as bad as in seventy-four. We will get through this together. However, in the future, you will wait to include your mother and me with a decision as big as this one."

Daylight brought the first glimpse of what was left of the farm. Chickens were everywhere, as were the cows. The horses had apparently run off.

Neighbors were standing in our yard in silence. They started arriving with food.

"Children first, please come eat."

I knew for sure that I was on the verge of starvation. My stomach growled all night. The taste of home-baked bread satisfied me enough, smothered in freshly churned butter. I did not even need to put jam, jelly, or honey on it today.

After everyone was fed, the men assessed the damage to the barn and house. The beams holding up the house were weak due to the fire.

A knowledgeable man had arrived from town and said that the house could collapse at any moment. Small groups of men would be let inside to see what belongings would be saved.

"It will depend on the structure, as to how long we can stay inside."

Another person announced that bedding and clothing could be repaired. They reeked of smoke, and some were covered in soot.

Mama cried when she passed her family bible down the line. It was the first item that was not bedding or clothing to be saved.

We were laying everything out on the ground. Teacups, plates, cooking utensils were all saved.

I jumped for joy when I passed Sass-A-Frass down the line. She was dirty, but otherwise in good shape.

When we were finished, the ladies gathered the wash to take home.

Daddy decided that he and George would stay behind while the rest of us went to the neighbor's home to stay. Johnny and Bertie had nothing to do with being sent away. After much thought, daddy agreed to them staying behind. Mama had whispered something into daddy's ear right before he gave his consent.

The four of us women left the farm.

A government man appeared a short time after the fire. It was as if the vultures were coming out of nowhere.

Daddy had to attend a hearing in Wichita regarding the homestead.

He was hopeful when he left, but the whole town was on pins and needles. Everyone knew that his fate could soon be theirs. He put in four years and ten months towards ownership out of the required five. Would the man be lenient?

Daddy told us he sat quietly as the man announced that the terms of the homestead agreement had not been met. He said that the sound of the gavel coming down hard on the table rang in his ear for hours. He hung his head as the man announced that the farm was now the property of the US Government. It would be given to another family hoping for land ownership.

Daddy was devastated and felt as if his world was over when he left the courthouse. What would happen to his family now? Where would they go? They could return to their family in Michigan. It was an option, but not one that he liked. Go home a defeated man.

The man stopped him to inquire if he had heard about land in New Mexico that could be turned into a cattle ranch. He said it was like a heavenly being in a man's body just waiting for him.

It turns out he was a man from the railroad trying to get people interested in moving farther west.

When daddy returned to us, he announced that we would be moving. He knew that it was a sign from God. Mama knew she did not win the battle to move back to Michigan. It did not surprise her because she knew her husband all too well.

What was left of our belongings was packed into the wagon. Luckily, the neighbors found our horses.

We took two cows with us for milk along the trail. It was early August and it would take us six to eight weeks of travel to reach the "Land of Enchantment," as it was called by the real estate developers.

George rode on horseback up ahead of us. He would leave us a sign on a tree or shrub indicating he was well. It became a game for the youngest of us to spot the piece of cloth he left behind. At times, we would all three see it at the same time, and we would race to get to it first.

It seemed to me that all I did was walk. The wagons were loaded with just enough room to sleep.

A couple of other families decided to follow us. The grasshoppers won this time.

It was near the end of October when we pulled our wagons into a small railroad town some sixty miles west of Albuquerque, known as McCarty's Station, New Mexico. There were mountains off in the distance, with snow on their peaks and sandstone cliffs surrounding the area. It was as if we were in a bowl. As usual, in New Mexico, a Catholic Church sat perched on top of the hill for all to see.

My first sight of the area was a little Mexican lady sweeping the dirt with her straw broom. I stared at her, only because I had never seen dirt swept as neat and clean. The dirt was beaten down so smoothly that it looked to be a floor.

Daddy did have to work for the railroad as a baggage carrier and maintenance man, along with learning how to be a rancher.

Mama said that she did not worry about her younger children as much as she worried about the older ones. Young children are more adaptable, where the older ones are more set in their ways.

Nellie was beside herself, being stuck out here in the middle of nowhere. She had no inkling that the man destined to become her husband worked beside her father.

As I cuddled Sassy that first night in our new town, I said:

Sassy,
We have been through dogs tearing you to pieces to hordes of grasshoppers. What will we see next? I am not worried because I have you to tell my troubles to; you always listen.
Good night, Sassy, I love you.

A family that rides out the tough times together gets that much stronger.

DIA de Los MUERTOS
The picture is property of JK Hoffman

CHAPTER 4

Dia De Los Muertos

McCarty's Station, New Mexico~
October-November 1883
Age~7

"Mama, Mama, guess what?" Shouted Lizzie as she came racing through the door and into the kitchen.

"Lizzie, go out the door and come inside again. You must act like a lady at all times. Now, go, and don't forget to wipe your feet." Mama mumbled under her breath, "That girl will make me old before my time."

Lizzie made every attempt to please her mama because she had something special to ask her. Quietly, she opened the door, wiping her feet on the bristle brush beside the back door. She entered, taking small steps and greeting her mama with a smile. "Hello, Mama. How are you today? May I help you with anything?"

"Why, yes, there is. Put the tea kettle on the stove and when it has boiled, make us some tea. My feet are tired, and I need to sit a spell."

Lizzie did as she was told, getting down four cups and saucers from the cupboard. She set the table with spoons alongside each place setting and a folded linen napkin. She rather enjoyed the ritual of afternoon tea with her mother. The traditional formality was intriguing to a young girl of seven.

"It is just the two of us today, Lizzie. Tillie is with Nellie, and they won't be home until suppertime. I baked fresh gingerbread. It is in the stove warmer. There is freshly churned butter out in the crock."

Seldom was it just Lizzie and her mother. When you come from a family of eight people, you rarely get time alone with anyone. Lizzie felt special, almost as if she could feel herself growing up right in front of her own eyes.

The two sat at the table in the small adobe house, enjoying conversing with one another. The kitchen was warm from all of Mama's activities around the stove. She had just learned to make the red chili corn tamales using the husks of the corn to the masa and pork inside its warm blanket. At least, that is how Lizzie liked to think of the traditional Mexican dish. This was mama's first attempt to make the tamales after the corn harvest by herself. She had instruction from the ladies in town.

"I watched Senora Lopez make tamales today, Mama. There were several women gathered around the big outdoor plaza, and they talked and laughed as they were working. It looked as if they were having so much fun working. How can that be, Mama? Doesn't work, like cooking mean that you have to be serious?"

"I am sorry, Lizzie, that I have not shared with you the stories of my youth. If only you could have seen the merriment in my town in Germany. All the women in town would gather together to cook for large gatherings or to sew. They would all tend to the children. We children loved those days when we could be together frolicking in the town. It was such a feeling of freedom for us. Now, tell me what you wanted to say earlier. I am very curious."

"Senora Lopez has asked if I could accompany their family to the *Dia de Los Muertos* celebration next week."

"What on earth is a *Dia de Los Muertos* celebration?"

"It is a time to celebrate the lives of people who have lived before us. You know, our loved ones. The families gather at the cemeteries where their ancestors are buried and have festivities for the dead. It is their way of celebrating the lives of their ancestors. It is a festival which goes on for several days."

"My friend, Maria, said that she has so much fun, and she could not believe that we do not celebrate our dead ancestors. Mama, I did not know what to tell her. She thought it was a Catholic ritual and that I should know about it in my family. I told her that no one in our family was dead. She could not believe how we could escape death. She asked me if we paid the devil to live long, healthy lives. I protested at the absurd notion that we would pay the devil for favors. Do we have dead relatives?"

"Yes, of course. I do not like to discuss death, as we may jinx our good fortune. Different cultures have their own celebrations. Besides, we have had relatives die. No one escapes that. Would you be afraid to go to this celebration?"

"Oh, no," I said, munching on the fresh gingerbread. "Maria said that it is a colorful, festive tradition. I guess they do wear masks that look like skulls. Please, may I go with them?"

"I will talk to Senora Lopez."

I knew I would have to wait to find out. I was so anxious; I could barely stand it.

Maria told me a few days later that she heard my mama say yes.

"Don't tell her I told you. Act surprised. Parents like to keep us in suspense. If we brag that we know, they could change their mind. Be humble."

I did just as Maria suggested. Mama did not immediately tell me yes. I had to sit quietly and listen to everything that could possibly happen and why I should not go. I was getting fidgety in my chair. At one point, she told me not to twist my hair. Finally, she said I could. I had to promise the moon.

I packed a bag of a few belongings and kissed the family good-bye. We placed my things into Lopez's wagon. It was loaded with food and colorful blankets. We set out to the small community northeast of us.

There was a procession of wagons headed to the festival. We would go to the graveyard by the church. Some men played music as we traveled. It reminded me of our journey from Kansas.

The steeple on the Catholic Church was what we saw first. A Mexican flag was tied to the steeple. The red, white, and green colors flew proudly over the plaza.

I asked what the decoration in the middle was.

"It is an eagle, sitting on a cactus devouring a rattlesnake. The ancients believed that if they found an eagle perched on a cactus eating a rattler, it was a lucky place to live, and they would be prosperous there."

We jumped down from the wagon and eagerly helped unload. No one had to be told what to do.

Many people were gathering for the festival. Maria and I became very excited.

Luckily, my black hair and dark eyes made me less conspicuous; especially when I put on my black lace mantilla and a red blouse with a frilly collar and a twirly skirt of red, orange, and green. Maria and I spun or skirts around and around. I felt very festive.

We set up a canvas tent and walked to the cemetery. There we placed candles, plates of food, drawings, and blankets around their family's grave. Men were playing guitars and singing beautiful music. There was dancing, unlike I had ever seen before.

The festival went on into the early-morning hours. Maria and I returned to the tent to sleep.

We woke to the smell of fresh tortillas, eggs, and beans cooking on the fire. We were hungry.

We were told to go to the well and bring water back. Maria took a long pole and two buckets for her, and she handed me a bucket.

"Just one for me? I can carry two." I protested, wanting to do my part.

"Have you ever carried two buckets of water on your shoulders, *mi Amiga Mujer*?"

"No, but let me try. *Por favor*?"

We filled the buckets and steadied the pole across my shoulders. Maria placed one bucket. My shoulder bent towards the ground.

"It will be better when I get the second one placed," she explained.

"Are you loco?" I asked. "I can't even hold this one up without spilling it."

"Wait and see, hold still."

She placed the second one, and it did balance me out better, but I was still not steady on my feet. There were others there at the well. I was the only one having trouble. I am not a quitter. First, I practiced with small steps, gradually getting the hang of it. Success! I did it, and there was still a little water left in the buckets when we arrived back at the tent.

"It is okay," her mama said. "Now, go back for more. *Darce prisa*."

"What does *darce prisa* mean?"

"Make it quick. *Madre* needs water to steam the tamales. They are steamed in a large pot of water over the fire. Our ancestors love tamales."

That evening the celebrations went on.

We got the nerve to dance. Maria was showing me how, when suddenly, the bells in the church tower started to make a bong sound. Someone was trying to get everyone's attention.

The music stopped, and we gathered around a man in the middle of the square. A white man with a bandana over his face. Then I noticed several more men with guns. They appeared seemingly out of nowhere.

"We are not here to hurt anyone," he announced. "Just cooperate with us, and everyone will be fine." He pranced around the plaza displaying his gun.

I could hear the whispers of *"Bandidos"* in the crowd. Outlaws. Maria was scared. Her dark skin turned pale. She began shaking.

It was all she could do to hold back her tears.

"Now, Senora's get my men and me some food. We could smell it for miles. We are hungry. You Senor, you are to help my men get the horses hidden in the barn. Feed them hay for they haven't eaten today."

The poor man shook his head yes and went off with a couple of the bandits.

The crowd froze when a shot was heard near the barn.

"Well, I guess somebody didn't listen and do as they were told. Listen up, do as we say. You, over there in the red blouse sitting on the bench, get me something to drink."

Me! Was he talking to me? I got up and started to go to the well. A heavy hand came down on my shoulder, stopping me in my tracks.

"Chica estupida. No agua. Tequila." He yelled at me, thinking I could understand.

Luckily for me, Senora Lopez brought him a jug filled with strong liquor.

Just as I thought I was done with him, he told me to follow him and his men. He also grabbed a young man. We were their hostages to protect them while they were here. They tied our hands together, and we were back to back.

Is all I could think of was that I was glad it was me and not Maria. Poor thing, she could get us all killed.

The men drank for what seemed like hours. Demanding more liquor. The hours went on, and the boy and I had a difficult time staying awake. I would fall asleep and nearly tumbled over, and then he would sit up, bringing me back upright. This went on for several hours.

There was a commotion outside. My blood turned cold with fright. I tried getting my hand loose. The boy realized what I was doing, and he began moving his back and forth.

The men came and grabbed their guns. They were in a drunken stupor, stumbling around in the dark.

We realized that we were surrounded by a posse. Help came. The banditos did not surrender without a fight.

Shots were being fired all around us. Our hands finally got loose. It was daylight, and I could see the empty jug lying on the ground. One of the outlaws was crouched near the ground in front of me with a gun in his hand. My mind pictured me slowly reaching for the jug and aiming it for his head. It was a risk. If I missed, he might harm me. I went for it. I held on to that jug so hard that it broke in two when it hit his head. He was out cold.

Before I could comprehend what I had just done, I was grabbed from behind and thrown over someone's shoulder. I was fighting mad at this time. I had been laughed at, tied up, forced to listen to braggarts all night, hit a man over the head, and now I was carried like a bean sack over someone's shoulder. I had enough.

As he went to put me down, I slugged him right in the jowls.

"Dang, Lizzie, it's me, Bertie. I just saved you, and you punched me hard, girl."

"Oh, Bertie, I am so sorry. I thought it was one of them. Are you alright?"

"I will be, sis, how about you? You were good out there. I am proud of my little sister."

"Thanks, Bertie. I am glad it was you who threw me over your shoulders and not one of them."

The outlaws were gathered and taken to the nearest jail.

I was introduced to the boy I was tied up with. It was good to put a face with him.

We were hungry and tired after our long night. We ate tamales, beans, eggs, and warm tortillas. It was the best breakfast.

I gathered my belongings and said Adios to my new family and friends. It would be a 'Day of the Dead' I would never forget.

I sat behind Bertie on his horse, and we headed home.

I could hear them saying, "Hasta La Vista. Lizzie," as we rode off.

Sassy,
You will never believe what a good time I had on the Day of the Dead festival. We danced and sang songs. I carried two buckets of water on my shoulders. Oh, and I got tied up by bandits, and I hit one over the head with a jug. I can't wait until next year.
Goodnight Sassy. I love you.

It is wise to know who you are hitting in the jaw before you throw the punch.

CHAPTER 5

A Marriage in the Family

McCarty's Station, New Mexico
June~1884
Age~7

Nellie is seventeen and is the most beautiful girl I have ever seen. Her dark black hair is as thick as wool on a lamb. Mama says that if she were back in Monroe, Michigan (where the family started out in America), she would be the 'belle of the ball.' That means that she would be popular at all social events. In other words, the boys would be batty over her. Her manners are excellent. She has etiquette and charm. It is not that she has been in many social settings; it is a natural characteristic.

Long before you become engaged to be married, you must first be courted by a man. This is a drawn-out process of getting to know one another. I guess you have to see if you are compatible with one another. It seems like way too much trouble for me.

Tillie and I have been watching this process with Nellie for a few weeks now. We first became aware of something different in her.

At first, she started to take more time to get ready to go out. She changed her hairstyle and added a red rouge to her cheeks. Her walk, her talk, and the way she dressed.

One day, we walked past her room and heard her practicing laughing. We could not ignore this performance. We placed ourselves on the floor outside her door. Not only was she giggling rather foolishly, but she was also pretending to speak to someone. We would hear her say, "Well. Hello William, how are you today, my darling?" We could not stay to watch her because we could no longer hold back our laughs. If she caught us, she would be mad as a swarm of bees.

We went outside and laughed and laughed. One of the men walked by and asked us why we were laughing, and we couldn't tell him because we could not stop.

How very odd. Nellie has never acted this way before now. Is she daft? Has she been tainted with some rare blight set upon her brain? Having older brothers, we have never seen them act as odd as she. Women have different conditions than men. Tillie and I miss the old Nellie. We hope she comes back as her real self again.

We could not contain ourselves when she began to sing to her hand mirror. Our giggles distracted her, and she came off her stool as if she were chasing a bobcat. We knew that we were her target. We ran out the door screaming with her after us. She stopped short when she saw mama coming from the parlor.

"Mama, you must do something with those little hellions. I have no privacy." Tears began to roll down her face as if some opened the floodgates.

"Calm down, Nellie. You do not wish for William to see you with a red, blotchy face."

We took our places within hearing distance of the two women. We looked over at one another and both mouthed, "William?" We know a William; he is the station agent for the Atchison and Topeka Railroad. He teases us profusely. We have heard talk that he is a very eligible bachelor, one of the few in our area of the world.

"Our Nellie is courting William Connor? What does that mean for us?"

"I get her bedroom," blurted out Tillie. "I am the next in line."

"Not fair. I want it. It has a nice big wardrobe. You always get things before me. I despise being the youngest. Everyone treats me as if I were a baby."

Just then, Nellie came rushing out of the door. She put her head up as she walked by us. We giggled, and she turned to us and stuck her tongue out.

"I'm going to tell mama on you," I said, confident that mama would take our side.

Go ahead, and mama is on my side." She went down the road happily swinging her parasol.

We ran inside to complain to mama.

Immediately, she pointed to the chairs and told us to sit down.

"I think that it is time that we have a little talk. Your sister is at a point in her life when she is at the doorstep to womanhood. Many changes take place within our bodies. It will happen to you."

We both giggled because we could not fathom it ever happening to us.

"You may find humor in it now, but you may trust me, one day; it will happen to you. However, you two are both close enough in age that you will be there for one another. Nellie does not have that. Sometimes, being older is not always to your advantage. Respect her privacy in this sensitive matter."

"Are they going to get married?" Tillie asked. The questions kept coming.

"Will there be babies? Where will they live?"

"Girls, these are all the questions that I have no answers for yet. We shall have to give it time. Your father and I wish that all of our children find the happiness in life that we have found. Now, let us get started on supper."

"You mean if I have a male caller, I don't have to do chores anymore?"

"It means that you need a special time to explore your life."

The wheels in my head started to go around. If I should get a boy to call on me, then I will have fewer chores. Hmm, who should I choose? Should he be older than I, like William being older than Nellie, or should I choose someone my age? I will not tell Tillie of my plans, or she may copy me. It would look better if it just suddenly happened.

It would be a difficult decision, as none of the boys sparked my interest in any way but friends. I glanced around the classroom, inspecting each one as if they were an item for sale. I would have to observe them in other circumstances.

It was a futile hunt. If I were out hunting game, my father would say, "Just to pick one and shoot."

A tall, lanky boy named Josiah had recently moved to the area. I would catch him peering at me. A smile would come across his face when I looked at him. He would be my first candidate.

I approached him as we walked home. Lucky for me, Tillie had piano lessons today. Mama did not press me to learn an instrument. She could see that I was like my brother Johnny and had no musical talent whatsoever. As the saying goes, "Why whip a dead horse." In other words, give up; it is useless to try.

Josiah, being tall, took very long steps, and I, being short, could barely catch up with him.

"Did you need help with arithmetic today?" I asked, not knowing what else to say.

"No, remember my daddy runs the general store. If we don't know arithmetic, we get swindled out of money. I grew up adding and subtracting. Do you need help? I'd be right happy to teach you what I know."

"No, I do okay. I have to confess; I was just making conversation with you. Do you have a girl? You know, someone you are sweet on around here?"

"I can't say as I do. Not much time for that sort of thing; school and chores. I hear you know how to shoot really well for a girl. I got a secret; can you keep one? My family is Quakers, and my folks don't believe in guns and fightin. Would you teach me how to shoot? I mean under wraps and all. You can't go telling anyone. I just think that someone ought to be able to protect the family."

"Sounds okay to me. Pa usually likes me to go with someone I know. Do you mean you want to sneak out?"

"Yeah, but I would have to let you know when I could go."

"Okay, well, see you around."

A few day, later, in school, I got a note passed to me. I opened it as soon as I could. It was from Josiah. He can go tomorrow. I didn't write him back; I just shook my head yes to him.

I ran home and took a gun from the barn and hid it out near where we shoot.

The next day, I asked mama if I could go riding for a bit. I have been really good here lately, and I knew she would say yes.

"Be careful and be back early."

Off I went and met up with Josiah. It turns out; he was such a terrible shot that I had not even seen a girl shoot as dreadful as he did. His hands shook really bad, just having the gun in his hand. No wonder he missed his shot. He couldn't hold still.

"I laughed and told him that it would be okay: an outlaw would be scared a stray bullet would get him just from bad luck."

Another attempt sent the bullet ricocheting into the rocks instead of the bottles. The sound bounced off the rocks, making a very loud sound. He cowered down like he was going to get shot.

I had Josiah throw a rock into the air, and I shot it. I hit the rock with the bullet and sent it crumbling like small pebbles onto the ground. He just shook his head and said he had to go home.

I learned a good lesson that day; I scared him off with my showing off. He never asked me again to take him out shooting.

I guess for now, I will do my chores and let Nellie have her time.

Tillie and I continued to be interested in this courting thing. We would follow Nellie and William around town. Sometimes, they would stop for no apparent reason, and he would just kiss her; right there in front of God and everyone. One day, it was in front of the Priest. He stopped and blessed them. We overheard him say that he hopes their union will bring many children.

We went home and noticed that mama was actually giddy. There was an air of excitement.

When we went into the kitchen, we could tell that mama and Rosita was cooking up something special. It was no one's birthday.

"What is the occasion?"

"You will find out tonight at dinner. The Padre is joining us for dinner."

Tillie and I both looked at one another, and we both knew that there was going to be a wedding in the family soon.

Sure enough, the announcement was made and blessed by the father.

Mama immediately set out to make plans. They would be married here in the house. She and Nellie took many train trips into Albuquerque to shop for material for her dress.

Tillie got in on the to-do's and would look at Nellie as if she were the first woman to get married.

Daddy struck up an immediate friendship with William. He told him he could always use another man around.

On June 18, 1884, Nellie married William in a beautiful ceremony. Nellie was as nervous as she could be. For someone so happy, she sure did cry a lot.

It was a lavish affair. The couple received many wonderful gifts. I did not know that they had so many friends. A grand time was had by all.

Tillie played the piano for the guests.

Later, the bride and groom left on the train for places unknown.

I settled back down, happy to do my chores and be content with my life. Josiah and I will remain friends with our secret intact.

Dear LJ,

We had such a wonderful day. Nellie looked beautiful as a bride. Not that I have seen many brides in my life. She was as joyful as I have ever seen her. We are all pleased to have a new brother in the family. I heard someone say that there will soon be a bun in the oven. I think that means a baby.

For me, I shall wait a long time before marrying anyone. I did enjoy looking at all the presents.

Before you leap into marriage, be sure you are ready.

Lizzie's *Der Buhmann or Boogeyman*
The picture is Property of JK Hoffman

CHAPTER 6

Der Buhmann (The Boogeyman)

McCarty's Station, New Mexico~1884
Age~8

We women are to be included in the next cattle round-up. Tillie and I were excited to go on this important outing. We had not been out in the wagon since we moved to New Mexico. Everyone was going, well, except for William and Nellie. They were expecting a baby.

We traveled all day, getting to the cattle by nightfall. Luckily, the cowboys set up camp for us.

We ate supper cooked by the men. Tillie and I thought that was great. In other words, we were impressed by eating food cooked by men. Ranch hands have to cook for themselves sometimes, but farmers have wives who cook for them.

The night sky overhead was putting on a captivating show. There were so many falling stars, that I could not keep up with my wishes. Surely, one of them should come true. The clouds rushed by as if they had orders not to drop any rain on our arid desert. They were obviously rushing by to more deserving lands. The moon was bigger and brighter than I had ever witnessed in my eight years on this earth.

I lay in my bedroll on the cold hard ground. I cannot complain, even a smidgen, because I begged to sleep down here and not in the confines of the wagon. My parents were not eager to allow me the opportunity to try. For I am not a boy. Women stay in the wagon, protected from bats and snakes, scorpions, and so on. My sister, Tillie is asleep in the wagon with mama. I wish she were more like me and be more adventurous. I will make that wish on the next falling star I see.

I close my eyes and try to sleep. A coyote off, in the distance, howls a rather sad, lonely bay at the moon. That is what my older brothers tell me, anyway. I am finding it difficult to sleep. I am not afraid, mind you. I just did not expect there to be so much activity at night that would warrant my attention.

The rest of my family is gathered around the campfire, laughing and talking among themselves. I ask them if I may join them since I cannot sleep. My oldest brother, George, tells me that I had better go to sleep before 'Der Buhmann' comes to take me away. That is what is known as the boogeyman in German. I hate it when he tells me that. Of course, I do not believe in the boogeyman. I always tell him to stop talking about it and tell him he is fibbing.

The family ignores me and continues talking. I go towards my bedroll, shake it as hard as I can {scorpions could have crawled inside}, and then I decided to sit under a cedar tree. No one seems to be paying any attention to me.

I can hear the men talking. Apparently, a family traveling through the area had small children. A bobcat came into camp and stole the baby right in front of the mother. I shivered.

I sat, trying to imagine such a thing. I know that a bobcat is a fast animal, but to take a baby from its mother without the family being able to stop the cat. The men kept talking. My eyes became very heavy as I tried to stay awake.

A barking noise could be heard off in the distance. The cattle were very aware of a predator. You could feel their agitation. The cows seemed to be mooing as if they were trying to warn us. Where are the men? Gone from around the campfire. They must be gathering the horses to ride out and scare off the animal.

But wait, Bobcats do not bark. Is it a coyote or a wolf? Is there more than one creature out in the darkness? Now, I hear a growl.

"Daddy, George, where are you? I must warn mama and Tillie. I walked in the direction of the wagon. Did I take a wrong turn in the dark? The campfire is a bed of coals. No light coming from the fire pit.

The wind started blowing as if it came from out of nowhere. Hard wind blowing dirt into my mouth. I yell, but even my loudest voice cannot be heard.

Then came the rain and hail. I had nothing to protect me from this vile weather. Mama must be frantic, looking for me.

I trip and fall. My hands go into a cactus. Then as I try to get up, I fall into the cactus again. The needle stuck in my cheek. I think tears were rolling down my cheek, but I could not tell because of the rain. I raised my face up to the sky to wash my face.

What do I do now? There are cactus needles in both hands and my cheek. I fear that I cannot even get up without help.

There is a noise in the bushes behind me. What did the men teach me? Think Lizzie.

"Don't make sudden moves and don't make any noise." I can hear them saying. I just kept saying the words over and over. Be quiet, and stand still."

Again, the noise was coming from the bushes behind me.

I sat as still as I could.

Breathing, heavy breathing. What can it be?

I feel something coming closer to me, but I cannot see it. The darkness is protecting the culprit. I can only hope that the same can be said for me. It would make sense to me that he cannot see me.

Suddenly, lightning, followed by a clap of thunder, jolted me from my stillness. The light from the bolt ignited the sky. Is it a bear? It stands taller than me. A bear does not have horns on top of its head. At least for a few seconds, I saw it; I could swear I saw bull horns.

I began praying as hard and as fast as I could. Please, Lord, protect me. Let me see my parents again. Let me see Tillie again. Yes. Lord, I really want to see my sister again. I promise I will try harder to be nice to her, to everyone. I will obey my parents.

A bear with horns. A new creature that my brothers have not told me about. They are so good about teaching me how to survive out in the wild. Maybe, they have never seen such a beast. We have only been out this far west for three years. It must have come down from the mountains to the north.

Again, a bolt of lightning. Quick, duck down. Don't let him see your face. Don't make a sound. Where is he? Where did he go? I never heard him move. How can that be? Is he gone? Stay put; the rain is letting up. I sat for what seemed an eternity. My face and hand are throbbing. I could barely stay awake.

Warmth. I feel the warmth on my face. The throbbing is gone.

I am safe. Safely tucked deep inside my bedroll. Mama was busy cooking breakfast. The men were brushing the horses and saddling them up for the day.

Am I ill? Is there something wrong with my mind?

George came by and said, "Get up, sleepyhead. The day is half over."

I stopped him and asked him if there was such an animal that was as big as a bear but had horns.

"No. However, I have heard the locals talk about such a creature that preys on little girls who do not get out of bed and do their chores." He picked me up and started tickling me. He carried me over to mama and told her to give me double chores today.

As he put me down, the first thing I noticed was that the ground was dry.

"Mama, did that clap of thunder scare you?"

"You must have heard the gunshot and thought it was thunder. I wish we would get a storm. It is so hot out here. A good rain might cool things off. Now, get washed up so you can eat breakfast. I can use some help in gathering firewood."

I felt as if I was in a daze. As I washed up, I searched my hand for the cacti needles. No mark, only a scratch. I washed my face hard, trying to find one lodged in my cheek.

I must be crazy. I will not say a word of this to anyone.

Tillie and I walked out away from camp looking for wood or anything that could burn. There were tall plants that had several limbs that looked like spines. It looked like it would burn since it was brown and had no life showing on it. We broke off several of these sticks.

We went running back towards camp. As I was going by, I looked down at the ground and saw where the dirt was roughed up. I saw what looked like a track made by an animal.

Again, shivers ran through me. I desperately wanted to show someone, but I decided to stay quiet.

The night was upon us again. I began to get nervous. Tillie surprised me when she wanted to sleep outside in a bedroll.

I would be okay with her beside me. Two against one. What am I thinking? Should I warn her? Maybe it was all my imagination.

There were fewer cowboys around tonight. Some cattle had gotten separated, and they moved their camp to look for them. The usual evening talking and singing did not happen tonight.

We snuggled down into the bedrolls. I positioned mine as close to Tillie as I could, and I had sunk deep inside. My head was hidden. I closed my eyes and went right to sleep.

I was startled awake by the sound of Tillie wailing. My eyes popped open.

There, standing above us, was the monster. I could see his face; or was it a mask covering the bear's face? I could see the sharp claws at the end of his large paws. He was a substantial, heavy animal.

I was afraid to scream, thinking it would agitate him. Tillie looked at me with alarm. It was as if she could not speak. Panic was setting in.

I was afraid she would overreact. I held my finger up to my lips as if to tell her to be quiet.

The animal suddenly jumped towards us. We tried to run. Our bedding wrapped around us. We could not move. We were at the mercy of the beast.

He stood up on his back legs, glaring down upon our helpless souls. His claws reaching out for us as he came closer to us.

Again, I prayed, except this time as loud and hard as I could ask. I crossed myself several times. If he were the devil, he would be afraid.

An angry growl came out of his large mouth. The teeth were now visible. One bite, and we would be devoured instantly. Thick, ropy looking drool dripped from his mouth as if he could already taste us.

Tillie began to pray and sing hymns as loud as she could. Together we would stand. One of us might fall into his hands, but at least the other might be able to escape for help.

Are we to be a story told around the campfire until the end of time, like the baby taken by the bobcat? Would they say we were brave until the very end?

If we are lucky, someone may hear our screams. So, in unison, we began screaming as loud as we could.

His paw was coming right towards us. I could smell an awful odor coming from him. My stomach churned, and I began vomiting. He was making me physically sick. Then I looked over at Tillie, and she was doing the same. Was this some trick of his, to distract us? Like the stink bug or the skunk? Would he next be squirting venom out of his eyes like the frog?

I could not stop hurling, and the pain in my stomach made me crouch over. I began to cry endlessly. I lost consciousness.

As I awoke, I noticed a familiarity of the room. Why am I in my room at home, and how did I get here?

My eyes opened wider, and I could see my mother sitting in a rocking chair next to me.

My first words were, "Tillie, my dear sister, where is she? Is she safe, or did the monster abduct her? Why wasn't it me?" I began weeping.

Mother came to me with cool damp rags soaked in rubbing alcohol.

"My poor dear, calm down; Tillie is fine. She is very concerned for you. It is you who are sick with a fever."

"But the round-up, did we go on a round-up with daddy and the boys?"

"No, do you remember that your father decided that we shall go next time? Lucky for us that we are at home since you are ill. I spent too many nights out on the plains with sick children."

"It just all seemed so real. A bear with bull horns was just about to attack Tillie. I was so scared."

"A bear with steer horns would scare anyone of us half to death. Rest now, Lizzie. Your fever has broken. You are safe at home."

Sassy,

I have learned something about a fever; it can make things feel real. I felt there was really a boogeyman. It all seemed very real to me. Had I not woken up to mama sitting there telling me that I was at home, I would not have believed it. I think that it is George's fault for filling my head with so many stories. He likes to tease me about the boogeyman.

In Germany, according to Mama, *Der Buhmann* comes to children who are not behaving. It loves to take them away from their parents.

The Hopis and Navajos, along with many cultures, have a similar being.

Children mind your parents. One day, you too will be telling the story of Der Buhman to your children.

CHAPTER 7

A Lost Relative Comes to Visit

McCarty's Station, New Mexico~1885
Age~9

My parents began talking among themselves about a lost relative. Nothing is private in our house. It is too small for secrets, and there are too many of us around.

The idea of a relative being lost got my imagination going. Of course, to me, he was gone. He disappeared. Where could he be?

Daddy explained to me that this type of lost meant that they once knew of each other in another place and time, but they had not seen each other for years. Suddenly, Johnny had to make space where he sleeps to accommodate somebody else. But who could be coming? We knew of no relatives.

The day came when we were told to dress in our Sunday best. Then we proceeded to travel in the wagon to town. We waited for the train to arrive. We looked like statues on the plank; we were told to stand still and tall. Was it someone special?

Finally, the train arrived, and only a young man disembarked. His name is Jacob Hoffman, and he is my first cousin. His father is my daddy's half-brother. This family thing is sure confusing. He is older than my youngest brother, Johnny, and younger than my middle brother Bertie. Tillie and I are both smitten. We have never laid eyes on anyone so handsome in our lives.

My father made the only move towards him. Thrusting out his hand, he said, "Hello, Jacob, I am your Uncle Adam, this is your Aunt Josephine, My son, Johnny, my daughters Tillie, and Lizzie."

Sheepishly, he said hello. He looked tired from his trip. Then, my daddy began hugging him for what seemed like forever. Unfathomable to Tillie and me.

"I see you are wearing my hat. It looks as good now as the day I made it for my brother. It was made just before I left for the war. I wanted him to have something of mine."

"Yes, father told me. He said you would recognize it in a crowd of people. But here there are no crowds. Only wide, open spaces."

A laugh was shared between the two of them, leaving us feeling as if we were not part of the conversation.

He was holding one bag. I offered to carry it for him, but he insisted that he could manage.

We all proceeded to get into the wagon. Jacob hesitated before getting on. Odd, most men know how to get into a wagon. Johnny gave him a hand and pulled him up.

As we were traveling home, I noticed that his pants were not the usual denim or sturdy made fabric like we wear out here. They were dressier material. More like what William wore when he married Nellie.

No one uttered a word during the wagon ride. It was rather odd. Who is he, and why is he here?

Arriving home, we stood as if not knowing what to do next. Mama realized that we felt out of sorts as our guest. She gestured with her hand to go towards him.

Johnny was the first to try. Taking him to where they will both sleep.

We listened at the door, trying to hear what was said. Jacob spoke very quietly. We heard him explain that he had traveled by train from Michigan. Apparently, his father had contacted our father by telegraph, asking if Jacob could come out west. Jacob did not want to stay in Michigan and work at the family mercantile. There were too many children, and he would always remain a clerk. He stated that he was the youngest in the family.

My eyes widened; I am the youngest in my family. We have something in common.

"I have never seen so much dirt in my life. The house cleaners must spend their day dusting. How on earth do they get anything else done?"

Mama laughed and said she understood what he was thinking. She apparently still has days that she wishes for the green grasses of Michigan.

That immediately struck up a lengthy conversation between the three of them. George came in and apparently knew exactly who our visitor was. After all, George was seventeen when the family moved from Michigan to Kansas.

Jacob asked about Bertie. We were on the edge of our seats with that one. Bertie was gone from home for some time now. Daddy didn't talk much about him. Sometimes he would mumble and say about him having to go to become a man.

We were surprised when daddy started talking about Bertie. He told Jacob all about Bertie working for the *Aztec Cattle Company*. "Why, it is the biggest cattle company in the whole west. They are out of Texas."

I guess he is now proud of Bertie for being a full-fledged cowboy. I just wished Bertie had been here to hear daddy bragging about him.

We had a full, Sunday after church, dinner on a Tuesday. Jacob is special.

We settled in with our newest member of the family. He was having a harder time than us.

Jacob spent most of his days learning about ranching. He had ridden a horse before, but there must be a difference in the way they ride in the Midwest in comparison to the west. I think it was all the men could do not to laugh at him. I know they call new cowboys, tenderfoots, but what is below that?

Poor Jacob would be so tired at night; he often did not even eat dinner. He would be asleep as soon as he came inside.

He was practicing roping, and he kept missing. I could see what he needed to do differently. After all, I had watched my daddy learn from a 'Caballero.' I was pretty good myself.

"Jacob, would you like me to help you."

"That is right nice of you, little miss. However, I could not hold my head up if I had to be taught by a nine-year-old girl. The men would shame me."

I have to admit I was a little hurt. I have always been a girl doing boy things. I put my feelings aside and told him to go to a distance away from me, and I would lasso the cow skull. He could watch from afar.

I moved slowly so that he could see me. The rope twirled around in the air, and I let it out of my hand, slowly and precisely, with it landing almost effortlessly around the neck. I repeated it again.

When I looked back, Jacob was nowhere to be seen. I followed his footprints in the dirt to down behind the windmill. He was just sitting there.

"I don't think that I will make a very good cowboy, Lizzie."

"I watched my daddy practice over and over again. He loved to practice and learn. Is your heart in cowboying, Jacob?"

"I thought I could be one. If I give up, what then? Everyone will think of me as a pussyfoot. Just one more thing Jacob tried doing."

"Don't give up yet. I am here, and you can talk to me."

"For a girl, you sure are sharp. I don't think girls your age back home are as clever as you."

"Of course, they are. It is just that my life is probably a little different than theirs."

He laughed. First time I have heard him laugh since he came.

"I like your laugh. You should do it more often." I said as I walked away.

Johnny saw me talking to him. Great, now get ready; here comes old smarty-pants.

"You are too young, sis, to be talking to old men. You keep away from him unless one of us is with you. You hear me?'

"You are not my parents. I don't have to listen to you."

Johnny acted as if he were going to chase me, and I took off, running into the house.

After that, Jacob would barely say hello to me.

"Did Johnny say something to you after the other day?"

"No, course not."

"Don't listen to him; he likes to cause a ruckus."

Just then, I noticed that he had the biggest black eye I had ever seen.

"Did Johnny give you that shiner?"

"Don't want to say."

"Does daddy know?"

"Would it make any difference? All the cowboys don't like me."

"Half of them don't even like themselves."

"Now, where did you hear that from, little miss?"

"Around. I hear lots of things."

"What have you heard about me?"

"Just that you got in some kinda girl trouble back home. That is why you decided to come west."

"Sometimes, a man can't grow up if stays where he's been. He has to leave to see what he has left behind. I think I made a terrible mistake by leaving. Then, on the other hand, I now know what I want. I would have never seen it at home, right in front of my eyes, too."

"Is it a girl? You can tell me. I won't spill the beans."

He smiled and excused himself. He headed right to my father and told him something.

The next day, we were saying our good-byes to him. He was going home to Michigan to get back the girl he left behind.

"He didn't even stay long enough to get his bed dirty," Mama complained.

"Lizzie, stop spying on people," Nellie said as she came in the door. "My land girl, I thought I spied on people, but I was not as good as you."

I often think about him and wonder if he found what he was looking for.

Sass-a-frass,

Do Tillie and Nellie say that I had a crush on Jacob? What do you think? He was awful cute. Did I tell you about his dimples? They were as deep as I have ever seen. Those dark eyes, you felt as if he could see all the way through you, and his laugh; I just love his laugh.

Don't say it, I know. My first crush. Why are my cheeks turning red?

Is a first crush just for practice? They say you never forget your first love. I hope I don't forget.

WRITING JOURNAL
PICTURE IS PROPERTY OF JK HOFFMAN

CHAPTER 8

Tenth Birthday

McCarty's Station, New Mexico~1886
Age~10

Life has a way of throwing us some hard jabs. At times, it feels as though you have been thrown a punch right in the middle of your stomach.

Every time we traveled to Albuquerque, Tillie and I talked the parents into going to this curious shop near the train station. When the whole family used to go with us, the boys always complained and then daddy, and they would walk next door to the tobacco shop. I could not blame them, as I love the smell of fresh cigars and pipe tobacco before it is lit. Daddy would buy them for all the men, including Johnny. He smoked, but it was a secret between the men. Daddy knew that mama would protest, saying, "Johnny is too young."

Johnny is fifteen, almost a man. He could fight at war. It would not be much longer that daddy would pretend to treat him as a boy to satisfy mama.

We girls would look and look at the curious shop. Tourists from the East would swarm into the shop looking for that special gift to take back home with them. They had moccasins, blankets, arrowheads, and rocks carved by the ancients. Beads and jewelry were plentiful.

What I liked were the leather goods. I had picked a writing journal that I went back to and imagined writing in her. Tillie always teases me that I call it a girl. If it were mine, it would be a girl's journal.

We came to town on ranch business and for daddy to visit a doctor.

We walked down to a building that had a staircase going up the outside wall with a door to the top floor. A small sign beside the stairs said, "Solicitor."

I did not know what that meant. Mama told Tillie and me to wait. Johnny went on to the hardware store. He never hung around with us. He might get teased and then get into a fight.

"Tillie, what does s-o-l-i-c-i-t-o-r mean?" I asked, spelling out the word.

"Solicitor means lawyer. He helps you with legal matters."

"Why do we need a lawyer?"

"I overheard mama and daddy talking about a last will and testament."

"You mean somebody's gonna die?" Tears welled up in my eyes, and I could feel the warm tear rolling down my cheek.

"Everybody dies. Mama and daddy are just doing what everybody these days do. It makes it easier when the deceased is gone."

"I don't understand."

"Daddy and mama can say that they want the ranch left to say, George."

"Why not me?"

"You are a girl, and the land is not usually left to girls. Unless no boy is around. It would take a long time for you to inherit the ranch."

"Can we go for a walk? I am tired of waiting here." I said, much to my chagrin.

"You heard what mama said. I am not leaving. If you walk away, then you do it on your own."

"Not fair that Johnny can always go off on his own, and I cannot."

"Neither can I. You think nothing of me having to supervise you. It is always me who has to tend to you. Put yourself in my place for once in your life. Stop being so selfish."

"Gee, you didn't have to lecture me. I can't help it if I am the youngest. Put yourself in my shoes, Miss Know-It-All." I said, getting right in her face.

A familiar voice from the top of the stairs gave a stern warning by clearing her throat.

I looked up and saw mama.

"I just came out to check on you two. Good thing I came when I did."

"I'm thirsty, and I need to go find a water closet. I can't hold it any longer."

"Tillie, take you and your sister to the soda shop. See to it that she finds a privy."

"Come on, sister, you get your way, again."

As we walked across the street, we saw some boys in an alley. Johnny was there. He was on his knees, playing some games. We left him there, knowing he would be rude to us if we disturbed him. He would be embarrassed if two young girls hung around him. He told us earlier that if we saw him, act as if we do not know him. Of course, it was followed by a threat to be mean to us when we got home.

Mama and daddy found us in the malt shop. They were finished with their errands and were ready to go home. Daddy looked tired and was coughing. He tried to hide the hankie that had blood on the fabric.

Mama looked worried.

"Let's get home."

As we walked along the street, a fight was going on in the alley. There was quite a commotion. People gathered to watch. It was as if the one's fighting liked the attention and brought the fight out to the street.

We all recognized the shirt as Johnny.

Just then, the Sheriff walked up and ordered them to stop. Johnny looked up at him and turned around and hit his opponent right in the stomach. Then his opponent hit him in the eye.

The Sheriff was mad. He ordered them to stop again. Soon the Sheriff was trying to subdue the boys. Daddy stepped in to stop Johnny, and somehow the sheriff mistook him and hit him with his Billy club.

Daddy's nose began bleeding profusely. That stopped the fight in its tracks.

Daddy was taken back to the doctor's office and Johnny, and the other boy was taken to jail.

Mama gave us money to buy our train tickets home and sent us on our way. She telegraphed Nellie to say that they would be delayed but to please take care of us for them.

I knew that mama was quite distressed by the situation. She told Tillie that she would let Johnny sit in jail while she attended with her husband.

Mama sat by daddy's side all night as he coughed and vomited blood mixed with phlegm.

The doctor made a concoction of roasted black peppercorns, garlic, honey, and Indian gooseberries. They administered this mixture to him several times in a few hours. His symptoms subsided by the next day, allowing him to leave the office.

The two of them went into the jail to bail Johnny out. The Sheriff gave Johnny a stern talking to and told him not to return to Albuquerque any time soon, and if he did, he had better not let the Sheriff see him.

When the train arrived back home, people said that the two of them looked worse for wear.

That was a month before my birthday.

Daddy stayed close to home and rested. That put more work for the rest of us. Chores could not be neglected. The cattle still needed to be fed and rounded up.

I did not do my usual talking about my birthday. The tension in the house was high.

Johnny was worried about being responsible for the upcoming fall round-up. He was expected to pick up the slack for daddy and make the decisions on the ranch. He had never been put in command before now. He had always had older brothers around to oversee the ranch.

You see, Bertie ran away a few seasons ago to Arizona. He got in trouble with daddy and decided to move west. He got a job on a huge ranch in the Arizona Territory. Mama cried for days after he ran away. After she got a letter from him, she sent George West to try to talk him into coming home. That failed when George decided to stay and herd cattle.

That left Johnny and daddy at home to run the ranch. Daddy never trusted Johnny to have a lick of sense. They fought all the time. Mama stood up for Johnny, arguing that he was just a youngster…

"You protect that boy too much. You are going to do him more harm than good."

This was going on as Tillie, and I left for school on my birthday. No one said anything to me that day. I was feeling very sorry for myself.

When we got home from school, we did our chores, and we were told that Nellie was fixing dinner for all of us. This was not uncommon these days.

Tillie and I could smell the roast cooking all the way down the road.

We helped her by taking care of little Georgie. He was just two years old and a handful. He loved to be chased.

I did not realize until I went to the kitchen to get him some milk that she had baked a cake for me.

I could now get excited about my birthday. The family had not forgotten, as I had thought.

My first gift was a new bow for my hair from Nellie and Tillie. Then mama brought out what looked to be a book wrapped in a white paper with a ribbon. I meticulously removed the ribbon; thinking I could use it in my hair, also. I opened the paper cautiously, not wanting to tear it. We saved everything.

Before I could get the paper off, I could smell the fresh leather. My favorite smell. Then I saw my initials, EMH, in the book. I knew immediately that it was a leather journal made by my daddy.

I anxiously hugged my journal, thanking everyone. Of course, I gave daddy a great big hug and kiss.

It was my best birthday ever.

We finished with cake. My favorite, a white cake with a warm chocolate sauce poured over the top. The yummy warm sauce soaks into the cake, moistening it with a delicious chocolate flavor.

That night at home, I placed my Sassy doll where she could see what I was writing. I told her that she would be no less important to me now that I have a journal. I did not understand then that a journal would last far longer in a girl's heart than a doll.

I thought and thought about what I would write. The candle burned down to a nub. I had to write something. I introduced myself to my journal.

Journal I thought, I had to call it something other than the journal. I shall call you LJ. I was speaking out loud so Sassy could hear. LJ, it stands for Lizzie's journal. Your name is LJ.

I began writing. I was so happy with my present. Now, when we went to Albuquerque, I would not have to wish for the dime store journal. I had my very own journal, made by my daddy, with all the love for the world.

Mama came in and told me to put it away and get to bed.

I went to sleep thinking about what I would write in it tomorrow.

Sassy doll, this journal will hold our stories forever on its pages. I have the best doll in the whole world and the best journal. I love you both. Goodnight.

Whom or what you choose as your best friend, be loyal and kind and love it always.

SPIRAL STAIRCASE AT LORETTO CHAPEL, SANTA FE
PICTURE OWNED BY JK HOFFMAN

CHAPTER 9

Trip to Santa Fe

McCarty's Station, New Mexico~1886
Age~10

I guess you could honestly say that life around the Hoffman house had become difficult.

There was growing anxiety over my father's illness, which grew worse every day. Then my sister Nellie lost her baby. I, being the youngest, was protected from the worries of life. At least, that is what I have been told. Of course, I knew that many things were going on in the family. How can any intelligent person of any age not know when things are rough? There seems to be a fine line between inclusion and seclusion. Parents often think children cannot handle a crisis. It is out of deep and protective love when these decisions are made.

Everyone thought I was naive or that my ability to feel the dark cloud that hung over our house was just a passing phase. I am guilty of letting my emotions fester deep inside and acting out at every little thing. Let's just say I rebelled. It allowed me to get the attention that I so needed.

My daddy was not well. I knew that he repeatedly went to Albuquerque to consult a doctor. It seems as if he goes more often these days, frequently staying over for a few days. He is as thin as a bean pole. His pants are now cinched up with a rope instead of his belt.

He carries an elixir with him, and he can often be seen taking gulps from the bottle. I don't know what is in it, but it smells awful. I know because at times, I have taken the bottle to him, and I removed the lid and smelled it. Yuck. If it tastes anything like it smells, it must be awful. He is convinced that it will cure anything. The newspapers must think so, for they advertise it as a cure-all. Mama calls it snake-oil. Even though this particular one has no snake oil in it. If you visit the Chinese in Chinatown in Albuquerque, you can apparently get snake oil made from snakes found in China. Daddy says he might if this gets worse.

Mama also complains as to the cost, ranging anywhere from twenty-five cents a bottle to two dollars and fifty cents. She will often do a mustard plaster on him.

On one of their trips, I accompanied them. They were going to take me to the Loretto School in Santa Fe, New Mexico. It was not a punishment that they wished for me to attend a girls' school, but out of love and concern for me. My family had always been raised Catholic, and they were taught that the nuns were the best teachers. Plus, we lived on a ranch rather secluded from society. My interactions with people were limited to a few select townsfolk. Not to mention that mama had her hands full and would become easily exasperated with me.

I have to admit that the idea of going away to school fascinated me. The opportunity to be with girls my age seemed exciting.

The Loretto Church, run by the nuns of Loretto, was in Santa Fe for some time. It is a beautiful church, being known for the breath-taking circular staircase to the choir loft.

Legend has it; the nun's needed a staircase. They prayed long and hard to St. Joseph for a staircase. A man appeared on a donkey with only a small bag of tools. He built the staircase with no support. He used no nails or glue.

I could not take my eyes off the staircase. Never had I seen anything so beautiful. Mama and I gazed upon it.

Suddenly, Mama was down upon her knees, praying and sobbing. The nun escorting us immediately bent down and spoke a few words to her. Mama answered her in German. Together, they prayed. I assumed it was for daddy. I, too, kneeled and prayed for him to be cured.

We left mama in the rectory with the other nuns. We continued our tour.

In a room where girls were busy sewing sat a girl off to herself. Immediately, our eyes met. I smiled at her. One of the other girls glared at me and shook her head as if to motion not to speak to her.

As I looked around the room, the other girls were quietly talking among themselves. Maybe, she is in solitude and is forbidden to talk today. I have heard that it is common in schools like this.

I obeyed the girl. I observed many of the girls sewing or doing embroidery. I fear that my sewing would be far less superior to theirs as I do not have the time or patience to sit quietly for hours at a time and do nothing but put a needle and thread through a piece of cloth.

When we reached the girl, I could see that her stitches were nearly perfect. She created a beautiful garden scene.

I smiled at her, indicating that I loved her stitchery.

Suddenly, out of nowhere, she grabbed my dress and said for me to be wary of a man and a black horse. He would cause great harm to me. Did she mean the man or the horse? My mind flashed back to my early childhood and the Cajun woman in Kansas. She had seen something she did not like in my palm.

I had no time to react, as the whole room acted as if I had been spoken to by the devil himself. Quickly, I was escorted out of the room.

Then, as we were leaving the school, she appeared, seemingly out of nowhere. With great haste, she grabbed my arm and placed in it a black onyx horse and repeated her earlier statement to me. Oddly enough, it was as if this time, no one seemed to notice our meeting.

I stuck the little carving into my coat pocket, and we said our good-byes.

Daddy started coughing very intensely. Before long, I noticed that he was bleeding from his nose. Mama said it was from the dry air. She kept insisting that he needed to be near salt water like Lake Michigan.

One of the nuns told us about a doctor in town who could put us up for the night. She insisted on taking us to him.

I was placed on a bed with his daughters. Apparently, they were quite accustomed to strangers sleeping in their bed, because they all just huddled closer together without saying a word.

When I awoke, I was surprised to find them all up and dressed. Apparently, I was tired.

Mama looked tired, and daddy was sleeping. The doctor could calm his cough down enough so that he could sleep.

We, at the advice of the doctor, left daddy there for the day. Mama and I could spend the day at the plaza in Santa Fe.

We were in awe of the native people, both Mexican and Indians, who placed their wares out on the charming wood covered veranda of the Governor's Palace. They would display their wares out on beautiful colorful blankets. It reminded me of my experience at Dia de Los Muertos.

There were baskets, jewelry made from silver and turquoise, cooking pottery, and even pottery made to look like animals.

I was reminded of my horse sitting quietly in my coat pocket. I reached down inside and felt the cool polished animal waiting patiently.

I then searched each display for a horse like him. There was none to be found. Odd. I would have thought that it had been purchased locally. So far, it was one of a kind.

We ate local food. The smell of food cooking in the plaza was almost intoxicating. You could smell the masa, and green chilies being roasted on hot coals. How could you come here and not be tempted to gorge yourself? There was bread of all sorts and colors. Beans cooking over the fire.

Musicians played in the center of the courtyard. It was a very festive feeling.

Mama purchased a brightly woven blanket. We placed it down on the ground with the other people and relaxed, ate, and napped under the beautiful New Mexican sky.

We may have stayed there for the entire day, had one of the doctor's daughters not found us and told us that daddy was awake and asking for us.

We returned to the home of the physician and found daddy alert and ready to travel towards home.

The look on Mama's face was a relief.

We caught the train to Albuquerque. They sent a telegraph telling Nellie that we would be home on the late train tomorrow.

We stayed the night in the hotel, which was always exciting.

Mama and I headed out in the morning to do some shopping.

We went to our favorite German Bakery. As soon as we were approaching the store, I could smell the bread baking in the stone oven. Mama and I stopped and took in the delectable aroma.

We stepped inside and were immediately greeted warmly. Of course, Mama spoke in German to the Baker and his wife. They always had to get caught up on the families.

Mama's voice cracked as she told them about Adam. I could tell by the few words I knew and the tone of her voice.

I was told to go out the backdoor to find the children. I was excited to spend time with friends.

We skipped rope and played hide and seek. I went inside because mama had been in the shop longer than normal. I found her in the back kitchen, relaxed, and visiting as if she had nothing else in the world to do.

When she saw me, she jumped up and said, "Look at the time. We must go."

Our order was packaged and ready to go.

"Lizzie, I am sorry I forgot the time. We will have to hurry now. It is just that there are times that talking to old friends who understand you can make you feel so much better. They cannot help me, but they are there to listen to. I do not have many of those friends left anymore. They are precious to me."

As we walked the cobbled streets, I felt older, more mature.

Mama asked me what I thought about the school.

I decided to be honest with her. I liked the school, but this was the first time that I had seen daddy as sick as he was on this trip. I felt a little scared and did not want to leave him.

She understood and said we could talk later.

We gathered our belongings and daddy. Then we headed for home.

Dear LJ,

Life has a way of never turning out quite like we plan. Mama has agreed to postpone my leaving indefinitely. She said she could not bear to lose me, too. As for the horse, Father Marcus blessed him and prayed that we should have prosperous days ahead.

I have you, dear journal, as a gift from daddy that I shall cherish always.

May you have friends in your life to stand with you in difficult times and the enjoyable ones.

PICTURE OF LIZZIE HOFFMAN AND BLACK ONYX HORSE
PICTURE IS PROPERTY OF JK HOFFMAN

HEADSTONE OF ADAM HOFFMAN,
ALBUQUERQUE, NEW MEXICO
PICTURE IS PROPERTY OF JK HOFFMAN

CHAPTER 10

Tragedy Came in Two's

McCarty's Station, New Mexico~1896
Age~10

I tried hard over the next few weeks to be aware of others. I had not shared with Tillie about how sick our father had been on our trip.

She was a little narcissistic, too. Is all she could think about was "Why I was not packing up and going away to school?" Mama would just say to her that it was between her and Lizzie. I did share with Tillie about the girls and what she told me. I showed her the black onyx horse. Of course, big-eared Johnny overheard it also.

When I got up that morning, the house was quiet. That is until Johnny came in and started ordering me around. He informed me that I had to cook him breakfast. He made so much fun of me that I had doubts in myself and my ability to cook. I made such a mess of the kitchen that it was not recognizable. When Rosita came in to oversee what I was doing, she started screaming and talking in Spanish. Her hands were flailing around all about her. Of course, I saw the humor in her reaction, and she did not. I was immediately shewed out of the kitchen. Rosita managed to restore the kitchen to the way it was before I started cooking.

I think I was so worried about daddy; I did not pay any attention to the fact that Nellie was pregnant with her second child. I am sometimes oblivious to the obvious things in life. I always accuse my family of telling me that they ignore me.

It was fine with me. I spent the rest of the day doing the chores that I was good at doing. It was odd to have the house be quiet all day long.

That evening, when the men came in for dinner, Rosita appeared with supper.

Daddy thanked her and said he did not know what we would do without her. It was obvious to me that she had told him about the mess I had made. I was waiting for him to scold me, but that never came.

Tillie and mama were absent all day and well into the evening.

Daddy seemed tired and concerned. He kept looking out the door in hopes of seeing light from the carriage coming down the road.

I knew that they were near when daddy went out the door to help them inside. So, I thought. Instead, he went out to hear the news from mama first in private.

Tillie came in and saw me still awake and out of bed.

"Why are you still up? You should be in bed."

"You are not my parents. Daddy let me stay up and wait for you to come home."

"Then why are you not asking about our sister?" Tillie was bossier than usual.

"How is Nellie?"

"Nellie is fine, but the baby is dead." She said in a rather curt voice.

"How?" I asked, not knowing anything in the world about childbirth.

"It is not uncommon. The next baby she has will be healthy."

Just then, mama and daddy came inside. Mama looked tired. She never asked me why I was still up and not in bed.

I turned to go up the stairs to bed, and I stuck my tongue out at Tillie. She and her know it all attitude.

The next morning mama took some time to tell me about what happened. I thought to myself that I did not want to have children. Tillie, on the other hand, took it as part of life.

Then the tragedy of all tragedies came. Daddy died. My dear, dear daddy. The angels came and took him to heaven.

What would we do now? Who would be there to take care of us?

We held the funeral service and buried him in Albuquerque. Many friends came from all over. The Baker furnished food to everyone.

I must get rid of this horse. It has brought us nothing but bad luck ever since it was given to me. It was the girl at the school. She is surely a witch or the devil's advocate. My head was spinning as I dropped it to the ground at the cemetery.

Then the world started to go around and around. Was the devil mad? I will fight you, devil.

That was the last I remembered for a few days. I woke up at home. Was it a bad dream? I have had those before.

"Daddy, daddy, I need you. Please come here, daddy." Everyone rushed to my side to try to calm me down.

I did not dream that daddy had died. That part was true. I had gotten very ill after the funeral. George picked me up and put me into the wagon.

The whole family was afraid that I too might join the baby and daddy in heaven.

I survived being ill. Johnny tried to cheer me up by bringing me the black horse.

"You dropped this at the cemetery."

My eyes grew wide. I was stuck with that creature. I asked Tillie later to hide it for me.

Johnny only learned then the truth about the horse and the little girl I call the seer. He took the horse to the priest and had the horse blessed. That was the story from Johnny.

It was not long after that when mama announced that we would be moving west to Arizona. It did not come as a surprise since George and Bertie had already made it their home.

Dear LJ,

Life has a way of never turning out quite like we plan. Mama has agreed to postpone my leaving indefinitely. She said she could not bear to lose me, too. As for the horse, Father Marcus himself told me that he blessed him and prayed that we should have prosperous days ahead.

I have you, dear journal as a gift from daddy whom I shall cherish always.

May you have friends in your life to stand with you in difficult times and the enjoyable ones.

SAN FRANCISCO PEAKS VIEW FROM THE SOUTH
FLAGSTAFF, ARIZONA
PICTURE IS PROPERTY OF JK HOFFMAN

PART TWO

FLAGSTAFF, ARIZONA
TERRITORY~1887–1892
AGES~10–15+

Picture of George Hoffman's Farm in Bellemont (Roger's Lake Area)
The picture is Property of JK Hoffman

CHAPTER 11

Moving West

Albuquerque to Bellemont and back to Flagstaff~1887 Age 10

Life without my father was chaotic. It seemed as if all the adults were running around every which way without a lick of sense.

We no longer had meals together. We relied on neighbors to bring food to us. Luckily for us, we had Rosita, who lived on the ranch, to provide us with a clean house and laundry.

Mama would come running into the house with her arms full of papers from the solicitor in Albuquerque. She would sit and stare at them for hours upon end. Often, she would end up crying and falling asleep on top of the papers. There were days when her bed had not been slept in the night before.

George tried to return to Arizona with Bertie. He just could not bear to leave, mama.

Nellie was in no better shape than mama. Just losing the baby and then daddy caused her to be on the verge of tears, no matter what was said or done.

Tillie and I were responsible for little Georgie. We spent our days trying to keep him occupied. Two-year-olds do not understand grief, much less how to keep quiet.

One-day, George announced that he had made a decision. We were moving to Arizona with him. Mama seemed relieved. It was as if a great burden had been lifted off her shoulders.

The ranch would be sold. It may take some time, but it was a plan. William, Nellie's husband, could put in for a transfer to Arizona.

Nellie took the announcement in stride. It would be difficult, but not impossible. There were many people here in our small community who would help her. Nellie always did as she was told. She never wavered from that. Even if it meant sacrificing herself.

George purchased land in a railroad community called Bellemont, west of Flagstaff. It was a farming community, and he had plans of us all living and farming the acreage.

We had to go into Albuquerque for mama to finish her business before we left. We had packed all of our belongings into a railroad car that would be picked up after we were on our way west.

We stayed in the best hotel in town. Its grand wooden staircase was highly polished. I pictured in my mind how much fun it would be to slide down the banister. Of course, that's what I wanted to do; not what I did.

When I saw the ballroom, it made me want to dance. I grabbed Tillie by the arm and led her around the room as if I were the man.

At first, she balked at me. Then she saw that no one was watching us, and she relaxed and played along. It was a good distraction from the two previous months.

Johnny was too busy pouting about having to leave the ranch. He did not understand why his brothers did not want to return to running the ranch. Mama confessed that she did not understand it either, but we would do as they requested.

We escaped in our minds to a faraway place. We pretended to live within the hotel, and that the bellhop was employed by us. In ways, he inspired that imagination when he would speak to us as we passed him in the hall.

"Good afternoon, ladies. How is your day today? May I get you anything?" His hand would twirl with his two fingers pointing upward as his arm would come up to his elbow.

We would feel as if we had melted down into the colorful designs of the sculptured carpet on the floor.

Tillie and I would laugh for long periods with each other. We can't remember who said it first, but we both thought out loud and said, "I didn't know you could be so fun."

Then we laughed some more. We played cards and learned new games, backgammon, and cribbage.

One day, we asked mama how long we had been there at the hotel.

"Are you ready to leave?"

We both answered quickly, "No."

"We have been here for five days, and we will stay for three more. I have to get my affairs settled."

George did not come with us at first. He was waiting for the man he hired to oversee the ranch until it could be sold, show up.

He arrived today. Tillie commented on how he looked better than he had.

We were surprised when he walked up behind us, sitting in the library room. He was quite interested in what we were playing.

"Cribbage."

"Looks interesting. Can you teach me?"

"Yes." We were so excited to teach George something. You know how big brothers are? You can never teach them anything. They already know it all.

We told him the rules and, very painstakingly slow, taught him how to play. He would repeat what we said over but get it wrong. We would begin by showing him all over. It took all of my patience to teach him.

Then Tillie and I had to decide which one of us would play him. We flipped a coin. I lost.

When we finally got ready to play, Tillie and I were worn out. Then, he asked for the cards to be recounted.

We placed the cards in the crib. We began. George studied every move, and then he would change his mind. The cards ran out, and we counted the score. George loses. We recount, and I am confident I won.

George yells out, "Muggins." He then laughs and holds his belly as he laughs some more.

We both went behind him and began banging on his back. George had known all along how to play cribbage because we had never told him about Muggins! That is George; he gets more fun out of teasing than the playing cards.

Mama was just stepping into the room as we were attacking George.

"Girls, that is not ladylike."

"It was my fault, mother; I played a joke on them."

"If you don't mind them beating you up, I will go on upstairs."

"Yes, please do, I will let them teach me another game, so I can win."

We played the rest of the afternoon, with George winning most of the games. When he loses, he is kind of a spoiled sport.

The time came for us to leave the hotel. Tillie and I danced around the beautiful ballroom one last time. I felt saddened to leave. It had become our home.

Nellie and her family arrived just before we left. Like all folks in the area, Albuquerque was the center of business and shopping. She and mama had planned to meet so that mama could give her the necessary papers for the ranch. Well, it made a good excuse for them to see us off from the train station.

We boarded the train. I raced a cranky Johnny to the window seat. I won, and he pouted. Is there something about boys that age? They are either tough as nails or as sensitive as a cat when you touch its feet. I can't figure them out.

We traveled all day. George slept for most of the day. We giggled when a woman thought that mama and George were married. George is old. I laugh every time I think of that.

The woman gave mama a nice compliment about how young she looked. Mama sat up a little straighter and smiled. It was good to see the mama we know to come back.

When we arrived in Bellemont, mama looked around. There was a large open prairie, and it was snowing with the wind blowing hard around us.

"George, I will not live to raise these girls out on the prairie again. They need a chance to finish growing up in a town. We are getting on the next train to Flagstaff. As for the train car with our belongings, it can be taken back to town."

Poor George was hurt. Mama did not back down.

Can you believe that we boarded the next train and rode the short way back to Flagstaff? Tillie and I could not believe it.

When we arrived in town, she found a quaint boarding house for us to stay in until our house could be built. It was as if she had her mind made up, even before she saw Bellemont.

We just did as we were told, knowing that we would be with mama.

A new life was just beginning for us.

Dear LJ,

We survived our move to the Arizona Territory. Our new town is young. The buildings are all new and smell of freshly sawn pine.

A winter snow scene outside of Flagstaff.
Picture is property of JK Hoffman

CHAPTER 12

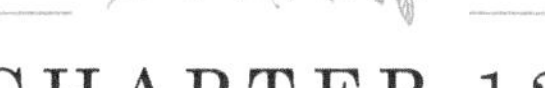

Butterflies in my Stomach

Flagstaff, Arizona Territory~1887
Age 10

Our first days were spent inside because of the snowstorm. We had snow in New Mexico, but not like this. We would look out the window at the blowing snow, and wondered if the sun would ever shine again.

The storm passed. Men were busy shoveling the snow away from the stores. All that snow, but when the sun came out, it was beautiful.

We got our first look at the towering snow-covered mountain that reigned like a queen over the town. I was instantly in love with the peaks. I would forever refer to her as my mountain.

Mama set to work arranging for our house to be built on some land she purchased just north of downtown. Construction had to be postponed until after the snow. However, Mother Nature cooperated with us, and we had a warm spring.

The men came around to help build. Johnny begged mama to let him go with them. He could get on with the spring cattle drive. She knew that he would not stay around us forever, and reluctantly she allowed him to go with them. She knew he would get hired on with his experience. Most tenderfoot cowboys had never even been around cattle before.

We were in our house at Easter. Mama was happy to be in her own house. She planned to cook dinner, no matter who showed up. The men always knew where they could get a good home-cooked meal.

They brought with them a friend. He had just gotten to town. Mama was thrilled when the young man said he was from Deering, Kansas. That is just up the road a piece from where we lived.

I first saw him when I was nosey, as to whom mama was speaking to outside. I did not recognize his deep voice and jovial laugh. He removed his hat and then I saw him. I do not think I have ever seen anyone like him before. He was tall and lanky. He was dressed up for the occasion with new boots, hat, and clothes.

Mama invited him to come inside. Suddenly, my stomach felt strange. It felt as if something were inside me moving or fluttering like a butterfly. I could not find my voice to speak. I ran out of the room.

I knew mama would think me rude and never understand. I had to muster the nerve to return to the living room. I spotted the baby kitten that had been hanging around the house. It would work as my distraction. I could focus my attention on the cat.

I knew mama would object to me, bringing the creature inside the house, but I did it anyway.

Just as I sat down, the kitten got away from me. My face turned red. Then the attention turned right towards me.

We were introduced, and he called me Liz. I like that. It sounds mature. Then he found out I was born in Kansas, and he nicknamed me "Cyclone." His name is Ed Geddes. Mama proceeded to tell him that I was born in a storm cellar in the middle of the cyclone.

That sealed it; I would forever be known as a cyclone to him. Is a cyclone an endearing name, or is he belittling me? Only time would tell.

I sat as far away from him as I could at the dinner table. Tillie knew I was disturbed, but I was determined not to share with her that he was charismatic. Oh no, she would not let me live that one down. Besides, I will probably never see him again, anyway.

The cat hid in the house. Mama asked me to please find it and put it outside. I looked all around. No cat.

Later that evening, as the men were leaving, he pulled the kitten from behind his back and handed it to me. He asked her name, and I blurted out, "Boots." He did not know that I was looking down at his shiny new boots. He apparently just purchased them that day. Did he know they were too nice to wear out on the range?

I was surprised when he started appearing with the men more often than not. Every time he came around, I would get those butterflies in my stomach.

We settled into our new life. I kept hearing mama say that children are so resilient. I suppose that we are. Me, I am just filled with curiosity and want to know everything that is going on around town.

The school was wonderful. There were no Catholic schools taught by nuns. There was not even a Catholic Church. We had to have our services once a month in someone's home. A traveling Padre would come around every fourth Sunday. It was hard to remember all of my transgressions for a full month. I used to have trouble every week at confession.

I made friends easily with girls as well as boys. Well, the boys were easier for me than the girls. I would overhear the boys talking about going out after school and doing fun things like shooting, skipping rocks on the pond, fishing, and hunting. One boy even shot a bear. I was envious.

Girls sat around and gossiped, played with their hair, and talked about clothes. I found it all rather boring. Of course, I could not let them know that. Especially when it came to birthday parties. I have never been to as many as I have here. If you do not give one yourself, you aren't fashionable, and you can guarantee that you will not be invited to the next one. Gifts are important, too. Store-bought gifts, not homemade.

One day, I showed my friend Catherine my journal, and she told me it looked crude. Then she went on to say, after she embarrassed herself, "Well, you did live in the sticks. It isn't your fault."

I was speechless. Never had I heard anyone insult someone so regally and get away with it. What was I to say to such a conceited braggart as her? After that, I hid my poor LJ away so that she did not have to suffer humiliation. LJ will always be special to me.

Boys would not be so cruel, I think. If they have a problem, they settle their differences with a scuffle, and that is it.

Since I cannot get into a tiff with her, I shall carry her insult with me forever.

Buffalo Bill Cody came to town, and there was a shooting match. I talked the boys into not spilling the beans about me dressing as a boy to shoot at a match given by Mr. Cody. I won.

Then my hat fell off of my head, and it exposed me for the girl I am. He took my prize away, just like that, because I was not allowed to shoot a pistol. Absurd. I told him Annie Oakley shoots; so, he gave me a picture of her. I should have had that, plus the money.

After that, Catherine never did like me. I was an embarrassment to womanhood. My indiscretion would not be forgotten or forgiven by the likes of her. I pondered my actions and thought that given the opportunity to shoot in front of Mr. Cody, I would surely do it again.

We attended the Fourth of July rodeo. We thought for sure our brothers would be involved in the display of roping and riding.

I spotted Ed. I got very disgusted with those dang butterflies in my stomach. Was I allergic to him? I had no one to ask who would understand. I would get them flying around my stomach like a swarm of them whenever he spoke to me, called me Liz, or even the silly name of cyclone.

I was rooting for him when his turn came around to ride the bull. He was barely able to hang on outside the gate. The announcer said that the tenderfoot from Kansas was down. He lost to the bull.

My girlfriends were surprised that he knew me. I impressed someone on that day.

After that day, I dreamed of him quite often. I would sometimes have nightmares about him and the black horse. I panicked that he was the man the little girl at Loretto warned me about. I had to know. When I saw the gypsies in town, I remembered the Cajun lady back in Kansas. What had she seen? I had no choice but to go visit the fortune teller.

I snuck off down to where they were camped. I had to return the next day to see Madam Xander. She took the scarf that I was wearing. How was I going to explain that one to Tillie, since it was her scarf?

She read my palm after I paid her money. Then she would not tell me what she saw. Did it scare her too much? I should have gotten my money back and a scarf.

I liked to read the newspaper. Sometimes we would find our name in it. That was always exciting. On the other hand, someone won the lottery from Louisiana. They would say when someone tipped their buggy over right in the middle of town. They would have news from all over the world. Mexico had a big earthquake, and lots of people were hurt and lost everything.

My teacher told me she thought I would travel across the world. That made me interested in maps and learning about the world.

Yes, you could say I was happy living in my new town. I won't change, even for Catherine. I am Lizzie and proud of it.

Dear LJ,

I have so much fun. Mama says that one day, my curiosity and tenaciousness will get the best of me. I am inquisitive. Do you think Ed likes me? I want to know. That is the only thing that really scares me... love.

Love has many facets. Are you willing to examine them all?

CHAPTER 13

Varmints

Flagstaff, Arizona Territory~1888
Age 11

The seemingly long winter was nearing its end. It was a winter with an unusual amount of snow. Some of the drifts were six feet tall. We made slides out of the snow, and forts dug into the snow hills. Snowball fights were getting serious as the winter lingered on. Then in front of your eyes, the snow began to melt as fast as it had come down. The streets were muddy, and we could no longer play in what was left of the winter snow. It became more of a nuisance than anything.

The days were warming up nicely. Mama told us that we would be starting the garden soon. I was at an age now when I would be of great help, at least according to mama. Tillie seemed to disagree. When you live in a house that is women only, you have to rely on each other. I enjoyed being outside working. Some days it would end up being just mama and I out tilling up the soil. We had to dig roots from trees since this particular area had never been a garden before now. We had to chop down a couple of smaller trees for the plants to get enough sun. We had visions of a large garden.

Everyone seemed to have the gardening bug. Of course, for most of us, if you wanted to have fresh vegetables on your table, you needed a garden.

Mama complained that this was harder to till than when we lived on a farm in Kansas, and we had a horse and plow to do the hard work. There were people in town willing to bring their horse and plow by and do the work for us. The problem being you would have to wait for days before they could show up to work. Their services were in high demand, and they cost money. After careful thought, we agreed to do it ourselves. We knew what hard work was like and also that there was a personal sense of great accomplishment at the end.

For days, we worked outside in the warm sun, preparing the soil. We cleaned out the chicken and turkey coops, adding that to our soil. It contains rich vitamins and nutrients that the soil may be lacking.

We bought seeds from Brannen's store and Hocksworth's Hardware. It seemed that the merchants had stocked up on seeds. We had pumpkins, squash of all kinds, lettuce, and cucumbers (we are all hoping for a big crop to make pickles…yum), potatoes, tomatoes, carrots, and many other veggies.

We got them in just in time for spring rain to come through and water the earth with a good soaking.

Mama insisted that two weeks after planting, we go back through and plant new seeds. This was a trick the old farmers did in case something like a cold snap came through and killed the first planting.

Lucky for us, we did the second planting. It was a night in late May when a cold spell came through and froze all of our plants. We went out to the garden to find the small shoots of the newly planted seeds frozen. Tillie and I were heartbroken by the sight. All of our work gone. Luckily, underneath the soil, in the warm confines of the earth, were our second batch of seeds, cozily waiting to sprout.

"You girls are learning what it is like to be farmers. You already know about ranching and how hard it is to keep the cattle fed and healthy. You see the other side. Ranchers and farmers don't get along because they are stubborn men who won't admit that one job is as hard as the other. They fight with each other when one is not more important than the other. That is why there are feuds between ranchers and farmers."

Tillie and I looked at one another in surprise. Mama does not usually, go off on a tirade over things.

She must have realized her outburst, for she apologized immediately. "I am sorry girls. Sometimes, I greatly miss having these conversations with your father."

We told her we understood. We missed him. Our lives have not been the same since his death.

"You girls have been a big help to me in the garden. I will think of a special treat for you."

Summer was going by fast. The garden grew quickly when the summer rains started. We were excited to pick our first radishes.

On Sunday, the men were in town for some much-needed rest. Cowboying can be difficult. Most days are spent on horseback, riding the range looking for stray cattle. Daddy always said it was a lonely job.

Immediately, they were impressed with our garden.

Our biggest problem is keeping the chickens out. Although, they do help keep the grasshoppers down.

Mama despised grasshoppers after living in Kansas. We had rows and rows of crops until they came in and ate everything. There was nothing you could do to stop them. As small children do, we thought we could help out by stepping on as many as we could. Johnny, Tillie, and I would have contests to see who could stomp on the most. Looking back, it was cruel on our part.

That is my biggest memory of Kansas, besides the cyclones.

The men promised to return soon to help us build a wire fence around the garden. The deer are coming in at night and are starting to help themselves.

Lucky for us, but not the deer, the men returned the next day. Deer are good scavengers. They can smell things we cannot. The wire would be put to the test tonight.

We spent the day pulling weeds from the garden. Mama says the weeds can soon take over.

We were out in the garden pulling weeds when suddenly Tillie let out an ear-piercing scream that could be heard all over town. Mama and I looked up to see her holding a garden snake in amongst the weeds she had pulled. Suddenly, the snake went soaring through the air. We belly laughed so hard we went down onto the ground. Tillie did not see the humor in what we had witnessed.

One day, a man went by in a wagon. The wagon had a sign on it advertising a special trip to Oak Creek Canyon. Mama stopped him and talked to him for several minutes. We assumed it was someone she knew.

Tillie and I were hot, and we knew that there was good swimming down there. A good swim right now would sure be cooling. The only place to go here would be south of town and turn east. I guess we would have to wait.

Sunday at church, we overheard some girls saying that they were going with the Riordan's out to the lake. When we asked them about it, they agreed to ask for us. Mama could not be mad if we were invited.

The answer came back, yes, as long as it was not raining when we left. There was no way to tell if it would rain after we got out there or not.

We told mama, and she said yes. Tillie and I did not want to seem too excited about the adventure, but inside we were jumping up and down. We had stayed at home all summer, and both of us had the bug to go somewhere.

The day came. We were up bright and early, packed a lunch and what seemed like half of our belongings. Mama insisted that we take with us dry clothes. Luckily, mama had kept Nellie's swim clothes, and I could wear Tillie's old one. It seemed odd to us, but she made us take our rain gear in case a storm blew in. I had gathered a few nightcrawlers last night in case we got to throw a pole in and fish. Mama would like that. She had wished for a fish dinner.

"You girls, be careful. Don't go out too far."

"We will," we said in unison as we ran down the road. "Thank you, mama." For as long as we could see her, she was watching us go down the road.

The sky overhead was as blue as it could be, not a cloud in the sky. We all know that when we live high in the mountains, things can change.

The fringed carriage was waiting for us. Tillie and I had never ridden in one with fringe. We felt very special as we made our way down through Milltown. The Riordan's owned the lumber mill and seemingly everything else.

When we arrived at the water's edge, we disembarked the carriage. Not wanting to seem too anxious, we followed behind everyone else. You could tell that other kids had been here with the family before.

We saw a couple of makeshift tents for us to change into our suits. We heard someone say that the water was cold.

Mama had told us often about swimming in Lake Michigan and that the water was always freezing cold.

We entered the water slowly, holding on to each other for support. The weeds had grown near the edge, creating a slimy feel to our feet. We giggled about it, but neither of us was leaving.

I saw the men building a campfire. I asked one of the girls about it, and she said they were preparing to cook our lunch for us. Land's sake! They are cooking lunch, too. I didn't know about my sister, but I knew I was just going to forget about my dried meat and eat theirs.

Lunch was fresh game, fish from the lake, and a variety of fruits and vegetables.

Some people took naps after the noon meal while others walked the shoreline. I took full advantage of fishing off a makeshift dock. The boys were jealous that I could put my line in the water and hook a fish. When I had caught six fish, I handed my can of nightcrawlers over to them.

The sky to the southeast was growing darker. Thunderclouds building. I was not surprised when they called for us to pack up and get ready to leave.

It had been a memorable day.

Having the day off to go swimming was a good way to get away. Although it just made us yearn for the treat again.

The garden kept growing until it looked like an unkempt mess. We were starting to get vegetables at a fast rate.

Mama was able to sell some to the local markets.

She came to us looking quite concerned. One of her customers had complained that it looked as if a bite had been taken out of a squash.

"We need to find out what is eating our vegetables. Obviously, it comes in at night and has a good supper on us."

Our heads went right to work.

We decided to go on watch. Just like the cowboys out on the range. We found a slingshot of Johnny's in an old trunk. That should do nicely. I know the men would take a shotgun, but a slingshot is much quieter. We did not want to get in trouble for waking up the neighbors.

The first night we sat together. I don't know which one of us went to sleep at first, but we both woke up at the same time when mama came out looking for us at dawn. No luck.

Whatever it was, had been there. We had to come up with a new plan.

We stacked some tin cans on top of one another at an opening under the fence. The suspected entry site of the culprit. That way, when he came through, he would knock over the cans causing us to hear him. Brilliant. When I asked Tillie how she thought of that, she confessed to reading it in a book.

It worked, sort of. When the cans fell and woke us up, we made so much noise that we frightened it off. We didn't even get a glimpse of the rascal.

We planned that tonight we would not utter a sound when the cans went over.

Success! It was a rabbit. We caught it and recognized it as the next-door neighbors.

Mama went with us when we returned the rabbit. We asked them to put it in a cage at night, or the rabbit would be in our stew. Mama was not kidding.

Unfortunately, it was not only the rabbit, but some squirrels had invaded our bountiful garden. George said he could come to shoot some squirrel for us. I reacted and pounded him on the back, yelling no.

Is all he said was, "Pound harder, and go up higher.

George is such a tease. We love him, anyway.

Dear LJ,

I guess we take growing things for granted. Until you have a garden yourself, you do not realize how much care it needs. I don't blame the squirrels and rabbits for wanting a taste of nature's wonderful bounty. They are not like us who can grow gardens. We are all God's creatures, and we can share. After all, they don't take very big bites. Now gophers, on the other hand, take the whole plant and run. Play by the rules, gophers.

Sharing, even with creatures, makes us feel good inside.

CHAPTER 14

Lizzie and the Water tower

Flagstaff, Arizona Territory~1888
Age 11

"Missy, I told you to stay away from that steer! You want me to tell your brother?" the scruffy-faced old cowboy yelled at me. I am not afraid of him. He is like that old dog that follows after him all the time, barking at anything that moves. He needs to shave his scruffy beard and take a bath. Despite his appearance, I like him. He has a kind heart, and I love that. Handsome and clean on the outside doesn't make up for meanness.

"George ain't got time to be hearing stories 'bout me. Besides, he won't do anything but tell me to find something else to do with my time. I won't you and I both know that, and so does he. Ranching is where my heart is; I will never stay away from the stockyards."

Jasper turned and walked away from me. I could hear him mumbling under his breath, "Damn, girl, makes me so mad. She ain't ever going to listen to nobody. Thinks she knows everything there is to know."

"You know, Jasper, I am going to ride a steer one of these days. Just you wait and see."

"Ain't no little girl ever going to ride a bull on my time."

"Johnny will let me do it when he comes into town. My brothers are all cowboys, just like my daddy was when he was alive."

"Don't go telling me your life story. I am not interested. I get paid by the ranchers to keep the stockyards safe. I do not get paid to babysit, especially some overweened little girl. Now, go home and leave me alone."

"Overweened? You called me overweened? I am not a cow. Besides, you look forward to me coming here every day after school. I overheard Bill Shroyer tell Mama the other day at dinner that you two were talking about me. Sounds to me like you two think I might become a rancher when I am all grown-up. You could teach me. I am a good learner, and I catch on to things pretty fast."

"Look, Lizzie, I am just a hired hand. I will be the first man there to congratulate you. Now, get on home before dark, and don't you set your Mama to worrying. Now, I got work to do around here. Tomorrow, there is a big load of cattle coming in from Winslow. If it were me, I would like to be a cat and climb up on that water tower to get a good safe view of the goings-on. You didn't hear a word from me. I have no more say than that old bull. Hell, I bet he has more to say than I do. I know he is worth a whole lot more than I am. If the boss man found out you were hanging out here, why, I bet he'd send me packing. He'd say I was too soft. Too many men needing jobs. Now, you skedaddle on home, and tomorrow don't come down this way after school. Promise me, Lizzie. Promise?"

"I promise, Jasper. It just ain't no fair that a girl can't have a shot at a man's job."

"Night, Jasper. Keep an eye open for cats. They can be pretty sneaky creatures."

I hurry home up Gold Avenue as fast as I can run. My mind is going faster than my body against the cold fall evening. If only I could get a pair of those denim jeans and a boy's shirt. I already have an old hat that I stuck back just in case. My brothers sometimes leave clothes behind when they leave town. Hmm, I wonder where Mama keeps them?

I slowed down the closer I came to the house. I did not want to bring attention to myself by looking disheveled.

I spied a scarecrow standing in a field of pumpkins. That's it! I will tell Mama that we need to put a scarecrow up in our garden. Oh, Lizzie, you are smart. Mama will have to find me old boys' clothes for the scarecrow.

I know I have to hurry so as not to make Mama fret about where I'm at.

I enter the back door of the house, and I kick the ash bucket that was left, apparently by Tillie, precariously situated right in front of the door. She knows me too well. It is my job to empty it after school, so she thought she was clever by leaving it in front of the door. Luckily, I felt it with my shoe and did not knock it over. She wants me to say something about it, but I won't give her that satisfaction. Besides, I have more important things to do than bicker with her about chores.

"Mama, we need a scarecrow. You know, like the Johnson's have in their garden. May I please have some old clothes from the boys to make one tomorrow?"

"Now, Lizzie, you know I have saved those for quilts. I guess I could spare a shirt and one pair of pants. It's not like it is going to get up and walk away. Just make sure I get them back. They are in that old trunk out in the lean-to. For now, you have your chores to do before supper."

"Yes, Mama. Thank you."

Just at that moment, Tillie steps around the corner and asks me what I am up to.

"Nothin, but wanting to make a scarecrow for the garden."

I think it best for tonight just to go about my chores as usual. What I want to do is race out to the back and look through that old trunk. Tillie might tattle on me and arouse suspicion. Best to drop the subject for tonight.

I drop off to sleep with thoughts of climbing the water tower and watching the cattle being unloaded from the train cars. I giggle to myself, thinking that most girls dream of dolls and clothes, but not me.

I waken, excited to pursue my adventure. It is early, with Mama and Tillie still sleeping. I begin my chores, even doing a few extra things to make Mama happy.

I wait for Mama to tell me when I can go out to the trunk. She goes with me to help me find the perfect scarecrow clothes.

While we are outside, Mama's friend, Bill Shroyer, appears. I overhear him ask her if she wants to go with him downtown. He says there are lots of people around to watch the big shipment of cattle being unloaded. Oh no, I wasn't planning on Mama being down there. I have to go now if I am to avoid being seen by them. At least, Mr. Shroyer will distract her.

With everyone going about their day, I grab jeans, a shirt, and a hat. Dressed in disguise as a boy, I run past people I know, unrecognized.

My eyes glance up to the water tower, shocked, I come to a complete standstill. The ladder up the tower is already full of men. My plan is ruined. Now, I have to make sure I am not recognized by anyone. I quickly reach down and grab a fist full of mud to put on my face. Mama says that women use clay to make their skin more beautiful. I will be a beautiful cowgirl! Wait! I better put dirt on me besides my face. That would look weird if I were not all dirty.

As I make my way to the water tower, I see boys from town. Will they recognize me? Only one way to know is to put me in their way. Success. No one said a word to me. Up I go. Never having actually jumped up to a ladder before, I fall to the ground. Be careful, Lizzie, I say to myself, don't act like a girl.

I get up and brush myself off and try again. I did it. Up I go, I cannot go very high, but I can see the corrals. If I can just hold my place on the ladder.

I am amazed at the view; I can see everything from up here. The mountain looks so big. I can see in every direction.

As I situate myself on the rung, I feel a sticky substance on my hand. Wiping my hand on the seat of my pants, I realize it is on my pants, also. I smell it. It has a piney odor to it…sap! Pine sap all over.

Suddenly, I am feeling crowded as boys climb higher, pushing me out of their way. So, to prove I am tough, I will step on the next boys' shoes with my foot. I am not mean, but really now, there is only room for one on a rung at a time. I wonder how high they are going up?

Oh no, here comes Charlie, one of the boys from Milltown. He is mean to me at school. I'll show him. I get my low deep voice on and say, "Hey kid, don't push me!"

"Oh yeah, let me by, or I'll fight you right here and now."

"No, you won't, Charlie."

"How do you know my name? You don't look familiar to me. You new in town? Are you from the Milltown? You ain't no store-bought kid, that's for sure. Something about you does look familiar to me now that I think about it.

"Really? I'm from a ranch out east. I just said Charlie cause that is what cowboys call a guy they don't know. So, your name really is Charlie?" I laugh.

"You sure do have a funny laugh for a cowboy. Girlie! Yeah, that's what it is, a girlie laugh.

My paranoia of getting caught was showing. Calm down and think, Lizzie.

"Now, girlie, let me get by, right now."

"Don't you call me girly again, or I will have to punch you." I could feel the heat rising in my cheeks. I was just so darn mad at him. I just knew if he pushed me, I was gonna have to stand up for myself. I was getting really tired of being pushed around because I'm a girl. To top it off, he didn't even know I was a girl in my disguise.

"Aww, is the girlie gonna cry?" Charlie was taunting me.

I decided that I would move to the side of the ladder as far as I could. But that darn Charlie couldn't just go past me and leave it at that. No, instead, he goes past and gives me a shove. To make it worse, he is laughing. That is it; I see red! I shove him right back. Before I know it, we are on the ground, and I have landed the first punch right in his face. His lip split and started to bleed. Then, I feel it, a hard-right-hand punch in the eye. The next thing I know is my gut feels like it is going to explode. My eye will be black and blue.

I let out a high-pitched squeal. Something about the way I sound makes Charlie stop. He looks right at me. His eyes so intent on me that I feel like I am on fire. In an instant, he knew exactly who I was. I knew I was done for. Our fighting had caused such a commotion that some of the adults were starting to wander over. If he lets on that he knows who I am, it will be all over for me. My life will be over. Mama will whoop me and make me stay home for the rest of my life. My mind is racing. How can I cover up a black eye?

Just when I am about to get another blow from Charlie, I hear a familiar voice telling us to cut out the fighting. A hand went on the back of my collar, and I could feel myself being picked up by the scruff of the neck.

"I told you, sonny boy, don't you go getting into no fights." At that moment, I was being dragged away to a corner behind a shed. "Now, squeal like you are getting a whopping," I was told.

Squeal, I do. I can't see a thing with my eye swelling up real big and dirt in the other eye. Who…?

As soon as I can focus, I see Jasper's old worn-out boots.

"Now, why in tarnation would you go getting into a fight with boys?" Your Mama is just right around the corner of the street. You high tail it home and put some witch hazel on that eye. I mean to go, get, and don't you go showing up here again. I mean it, Lizzie.

"Yes, sir," I say as I start to leave. I am disgusted with myself that I am going to miss out on the cattle auction. I bet Charlie will get to see it. Sometimes I hate being a girl. We don't get treated right.

Luckily, as I run home, everyone is down watching the cattle. I peel out of the jeans and shirt as fast as I can. I need to have the scarecrow up by the time Mama comes back home. In my hurry to make the urchin, I need the straw. Luckily, Mama had put plenty down to protect the crops from the cold nights. I grab the rake and being to stuff the straw down the pants. I am pleased with myself; I turn around to gather more straw. I step right on the rake with my foot. To my surprise, the end of the rake hits me right in my swollen eye. Of course, that will be my reason for the black eye.

I can hear chatterer coming from the streets below our house. I quickly run in and tidy up. Mama, George, and Tillie enter the house and see me sitting on the floor. I begin to cry and show Mama my eye.

"You have a shiner alright," George said, not making any attempt to show remorse for me.

"Isn't anyone going to ask me how I got it?"

Tillie broke in with, "This will be interesting."

"Someone told me to put witch hazel on my eye. Do we have any, Mama?"

"Who told you that?"

"I know somebody told me that, but I cannot remember right off hand.

"I'll get you some," offered Tillie, motioning for me to come with her.

I ain't scared of Mama, but Tillie can work the truth out of me faster than a bear can pull a fish out of a lake full of water.

"Who walloped you, Lizzie? Tell me the truth."

"I swear Tillie; it was the handle. I was making that stupid scarecrow when I stepped on it, and it hit me."

"You are the one who brings things on yourself. I don't believe you. Mama says she saw that shirt on a boy today down at the stockyards. I am betting that boy was a girl and her name was Lizzie Hoffman. I just want to know who hit you. Did you give them a black eye? Oh Lizzie, sometimes I wish I were as brave as you are. You aren't scared of anything, are you?"

"You are just trying to get something out of me that isn't true."

Miss Weatherford looked at me as if I had come to school naked. Yes, my shiner was three different colors, at least, and my eye was swollen shut.

"Oh, my Lizzie, what happened to you?"

I just wanted to get the parade of questions over so people would stop talking to me about it. It is as if nobody has seen a girl with a black eye before. I ain't the first, nor will I be the last.

Charlie walked into the schoolroom about then, and Miss Weatherford looks at me when she looks at him.

"Well, this is quite odd. A boy and a girl with shiners." Laughing, she says, "You would think that the two of you got into a fight."

Quickly I said, "No, mine was from the garden. I didn't get into a fight with Charlie."

Charlie looked at me curiously. The other children started teasing us, and Miss Weatherford put a stop to the commotion.

"Class, please take your seats, and we will not have any more of this conversation."

I feel Charlie eyeing me. Does he know? Will he give it away? My life, as I know it, will be over. How could I live this down? Not only is Charlie staring at me, but so is Tillie.

After pondering over my situation all day, I decided to take things into my hands. Daddy always said that if you want things to go in your favor, take charge of the situation.

"Charlie, I need to speak with you."

"Oh no, you ain't going to accuse me of hitting a girl, are you? My daddy would whoop me bad."

Charlie was scared. I had him right where I wanted him in the palm of my hand. At this moment, he would do anything I asked of him. Daddy would be proud of me.

"You and I are the only ones who know the truth." Did I just confess?

"I don't understand? It was you on the water tower actin like you was a boy?"

"Now, don't go putting words into my mouth that I never spoke. You just listen to me. We apparently have a situation where gossip will prevail. Now it is up to you and me to stop those rumors before we both end up with mud on our faces, so to speak. Are you following me, Charlie?"

"Yeah, sure, of course. But I need to know the truth. I knew there was something about you that looked familiar the other day. I was trying to figure out who you were so I could get even with you today."

"Are you saying that you want to fight me?"

"No, no, I mean to say if you were a boy and all. Let's just say, pretending that it was you dressed as a boy, and I would be looking to fight him. I am just saying."

"Are you good at keeping secrets?"

"Yeah, sure, of course. Especially with you, Lizzie. I would never tell a soul. I swear on my own grave."

"I trust you only because if you ever tell anyone, it will be all over this town that you hit a girl in the eye during a fistfight over by the stockyards."

"It was you! I knew it. I swear, Lizzie. Dang girl, you can pack a punch. Ain't nobody ever going to mess with you. You like cattle?"

"Yes, I am going to be the first woman rancher in these parts. My Daddy taught me how to punch cattle over in New Mexico. I even went with my family on a cattle drive to take the cows to market. I can herd cattle as well as any man."

"I have never met a gal like you before, Lizzie. You want to go with me to the pond and skip rocks?"

"I am pretty good, you know. I have three older brothers that taught me how. So, just don't go expecting to show me up. I will give you a fair shot."

"Let's go."

"It is pretty warm for a fall day, except for the wind. It might affect our stone-throwing. What do you think, Lizzie?

"Yeah, we can try a couple and see." I choose the flattest rocks I can find. My hand lets go of the rock, and it bounces off the water once, then twice, and again a third time.

"Now let me try. I bet I can get it to skip four times."

I held back my laughter as the stone fell into the water.

"I was just lining up my shot; that one doesn't count."

"I know I have to do that sometimes. You have to see how the wind is blowing."

"You are lots nicer than boys. They would be teasing me by now."

"They would be teasing you? Why I thought you and them got along real good."

"Nah, I have to act mean around them, or else they would be mean to me. I used to get beat up all the time until I started acting tough." I could see that Charlie was getting nervous with me there.

"Hey, Charlie, why don't we go home the long way?"

"Great idea, Lizzie."

As we walked home, we learned that we had a lot in common. I have to say that I am beginning to like this kid.

"Tonight is the full moon. Remember Miss Weatherford talking to us about it? Have you ever seen from atop the water tower, Lizzie?"

"No, my mama would never let me go to look at it. Young ladies have no business being out after dark unescorted."

"But I would escort you. I wouldn't let anything happen to you. Too bad, because I am going to go tonight, with or without you. If you change your mind, I will be on top watching the moon."

I mumble to myself as I walk away from him, that boys get all the fun.

I am distracted throughout dinner as I cannot stop thinking about the full moon.

Suddenly, Mama says that she will be out tonight. My mind begins to plot. There is hope.

The house is quiet as I tiptoe down the stairs and out the door.

I run down the street as fast as I can go. The moon casts a glow along the empty road creating shadows from the buildings.

Luckily, the steps of the ladder to the top of the tower is easy to see. I make my way up the rungs. Halfway up, I give a faint yell for Charlie. "Charlie, are you up there? It's me." I have to repeat it several times as I make my way to the top.

Finally, I see a head lean over from the top and say, "Yeah, I am surprised you came."

"I snuck out. I can't stay long, but I could not miss this."

"You will not believe how beautiful it is from up here."

"Help me up. This danged skirt is caught on some wood. I have to pull it loose. Oh no, I ripped my skirt."

"I see what you mean by girls having a harder time than boys.".

"Oh my," I say as I gaze around from atop the tower. "You can see everything from here. I feel as if I am on top of the world. Look, there is my mountain. The little bit of snow on top almost sparkles. I think it is the most beautiful thing I have ever seen in my life."

"Sorry for hitting you in the eye, Lizzie."

"Sorry for hitting you. But hey, we have become friends and that I would not change for the world."

"Me either."

Dear LJ,

I have seen the world from the top of a water tower. Well, not the whole world, but enough to make me want to travel and see new places. You get a different perception of things when you are up high. When we are on the ground, we can only look up or right or left. When you are up on top, you can see up and down and all around. I made a new unlikely friend on the water tower. That makes it special.

Sometimes, in life, we find friendship in the most unusual places.

PETROGLYPHS ALONG CLEAR CREEK
WINSLOW, ARIZONA
The picture is the property of JK Hoffman

CHAPTER 15

Petroglyphs and Ruins

Walnut Canyon, Flagstaff,
Arizona Territory~1889
Age 12

I love this town. You cannot get bored here. There is always something going on for entertainment. I haven't gotten to the Grand Canyon yet, but I will one day. Even in the dead of winter, the snow is great. There are four distinct seasons to experience. I am just so proud of where I live.

We are going to Walnut Canyon. They say that there is a real Indian Pueblo built on the walls of the canyon. I have seen pueblos in New Mexico, but this will be my first one here in this territory. I am fascinated by them.

Sometimes, I close my eyes and pretend that I am the person living on the side of a cliff. Dressed in finely tanned deer hide with many feathers adorning my long black hair. I wear beads made from the Pinon trees. I am always one of the hunters. I am neither boy nor girl: I am just a hunter. I stalk the woods for deer and rabbits. Everyone does work, and everyone plays together. We gather the tall grasses and weave baskets and make clay pots for cooking. At night, we sat around a big campfire with the drum's beating and stories being told by the elders.

Tillie says daydreaming is useless. I disagree. I can put myself as someone else. I guess for me; it makes me understand things better.

Today, we are riding our horses along an animal trail that makes its way along Walnut Creek. We have heard that there are ripe walnuts ready to be picked. I think this is the main reason for our journey today. Mama has wished she had fresh walnuts for baking.

We saddle up and begin our journey, meandering along the creek flowing down the deep canyon. Big rock boulders lie on either side of the creek bed. We lead the horses around the rocks, sometimes right in the water down the creek bed. Wildlife is plentiful in this serene valley. The white sandstone walls covered deep with bushes.

Our guide, a man neither Tillie nor I had ever met or seen in these parts, offered to take us to our destination. He warns that there may be poisonous plants and to be careful. I have heard of poison ivy, and apparently, there is poison oak and sumac.

There were fields of wild grasses growing where there used to be tall ponderosa pines. This was a logging area when they first began cutting trees. The logging roads are still visible.

We stopped to rest the horses and let them drank from the fresh creek water. We passed around pieces of dried meat and drink water from canteens. This was heaven to me.

The sky was bright blue with no clouds in sight. A light breeze rustled through the tops of the Aspen trees. The birds were singing, and a hawk was flying overhead.

We saddled up and continue our journey.

The guide was obviously paying his whole attention to mama. He showed her the many petroglyphs lining the walls of the canyon. We only saw them because they were pointing at them. The pictures carved into the sandstone wall looked like stick figures. I could see horses and deer and people. Although they were not new to us; we had seen them in New Mexico. I still enjoyed looking at them.

Mama and the guide rode ahead. We were not privy to their conversation.

Tillie was concerned for mama. After all, we had only seen her with daddy. This man who was paying her a great deal of attention was someone we did not know. Suddenly, I realized I was not happy with a man being interested in my mama.

We arrived at the first visible sighting of the cliff dwelling. It was even more impressive than I imagined. They had built their homes at the end of a pointed cliff. How smart these people were to build where they can see everything.

At the bottom of the canyon, we tied up the horses. Our guide led us up a trail, almost obscured by thick brush. We reached the ruins. A small foot trail led us around the remains of someone's home. Stones held together with mud still stood around a room.

We entered a room that looked over the beautiful canyon. The rooms were not very high; I am not very tall, but standing inside made me feel as if I were huge. Were they very short people?

I felt as though we were intruding on sacred ground. There were broken pots strewn around the room and carved stones lying on the floor. You could imagine the family gathered together for the evening meal.

As we made our way down the trail, a deer ran out in front of us, and a rabbit ran the other direction. It was as though they had been watching us, protecting the area. Quietly, keeping an eye on a sacred place.

We were not there to hunt but to observe. The animals could relax now.

We gathered our walnuts and other berries. Mama was like a kid in a candy store. There were more than we needed. I dreaded having to crack all of them.

We packed up and made our way back to town. It seemed as if the horses were glad to be back on the trail. They were feisty and wanted to run.

Tillie and I raced the horses down the trail. Soon, mama and the others are racing. When we stopped to rest the horses, everyone laughed.

I don't know when I have had such a fun time. Sometimes, it is good to get out and do something different.

I discovered that you could make a job like shelling walnuts fun. Tillie and I challenged each other on how many we could break open so we would have two perfect halves.

At first, we hit them too hard with the hammer. We tried several different methods. Once, the walnut went flying through the air, almost hitting kitty, who was asleep in the shade under the tree. We were glad we did not hit her, but we chuckled about it for a long time.

We were happy when mama came out and told us that was enough walnuts for now. They would keep longer if we only cracked what we needed.

We cleaned up the mess from cracking the shells, and our noses caught the smell of something wonderful cooking. Walnut German Shortbread cookies.

We both ran into the house and placed the warm cookies in our mouth. Yum. The shortbread melted in our mouths, leaving pieces of walnuts lingering in our mouth. Mama had a pot of tea ready for us. The three of us sat and had tea and cookies. We reminisced about our trip to Walnut Canyon. We planned our trip next year to gather walnuts

I was curious as to whom our guide was yesterday. "Mama, how did you know to ask that man to take us to the ruins?"

"George knows him. He introduced me to him one day down at the bank. His name is Bill Shroyer. He has been gold mining in Colorado for the past few years. He heard of the gold finds out near Prescott and the Grand Canyon. He has been surveying the area around here for gold. One day he met Mr. Fisher, who has a cabin down in the canyon. Remember the one we passed? The two got to talking, and he showed Mr. Shroyer the ruins. Mr. Shroyer was excited to tell George and me about them. He offered to escort us."

"George knows everybody doesn't he?"

"It would seem that way. For someone so quiet, he sure gets around. Mr. Shroyer then mentioned the walnut trees. I told him that I had wanted to make Baklava, but I needed walnuts. I am going to make some to take to the next dance. He said he would be sure to come and get himself a piece."

With that information, I was satisfied. Mr. Shroyer was pleasant, and he sure knew plenty of things about the area. He must be smart.

Before we knew it, mama announced that dance was coming up. I wonder if Ed knows about it. Will he be there? I will make a wish on that. Will my heart flutter when I see him? What does that mean?

The night of the dance came. The three of us got all dressed up and went downtown to the dancehall.

Mr. Shroyer was there. In fact, he was the first person we saw. Was he waiting for us?

Mama must have felt odd seeing him waiting for us. "He just does not know anyone, yet." were her words. Making an excuse when no one had uttered a word.

This time we received a formal introduction; instead of this is our guide.

As I watched the two of them throughout the evening, he made no attempt to mingle and introduce himself to others. He appeared quite content sitting beside mama. She appeared happy to have him to talk to during the evening.

Ed, on the other hand, came in with women on both arms. Not unusual for Ed. He had been sampling the punch a little too much.

I was disgusted with his behavior, as usual. He made his way over to me. I melted right into his hands as he asked me to dance.

"Cyclone, it is good to see you out and about this evening."

When I was just settling into the music, a boy from school came and butted in on our dance. "Why now?" I screamed in my head.

I wish Ed had told him no.

Then, before I knew it, Ed was gone. Women laughingly said that he left with more women than he had come in with. The women made no bones of saying that the ladies with him were sure mad because he took time out to dance with a child.

I am not a child. Besides, I met him first, and he will one day be mine. Mark my words.

Mr. Shroyer was still there. I could not even keep track of how many pieces of baklava he ate. He could not stop complimenting mama on her baking skills.

He was there to escort us home. Which is more than could be said for Ed.

Tillie said to me, "I think mama is rather fond of Mr. Shroyer."

Only time will tell.

Dear LJ,

Sometimes, even the simplest things can bring happiness. Mama, Tillie, and I rely on each other so much. At times, too much. When you can have a day away from your routine, it lightens the day.

I am planning on using my walnut halves to make Christmas ornaments. I have seen them on trees, and now we will have them as decorations. I think we are going to dip some in wax and use it for a fire starter. That would make a great gift.

Are the ancient souls still watching over their land in the shape of deer and other animals?

CHAPTER 16

The Baseball

Flagstaff, Arizona Territory~1889
Age 12

Miss Weatherford started the day with her usual reciting of the Golden Rule. "Do unto others as you would have them do unto you." We students had to repeat the saying back to her. Of course, there was the usual under their breath remarks by the boys. Miss Weatherford, like clockwork, would reprimand the boys.

One day I added the other saying, "What you wish upon others, you wish upon yourself."

"Very good, Lizzie, except next time, be courteous to the class and raise your hand before you speak out of turn."

A roar came from boys and girls alike. Obviously, they wished to be made fun of when they spoke intelligently. They completely lost the point.

At the end of the school day, Miss Weatherford asked me to stay behind.

"Lizzie, I wanted to apologize for calling you out for not raising your hand. Your comment was a good example, and I was too focused on our usual morning charade. I, too, need to follow the Golden Rule. Now, run along with home, and I will see you tomorrow."

The usual boys and girls were outside when I left.

"Did she whoop you, Lizzie? Do you have to write 100 times, "I will not speak out of turn?"

"That is what I had to do when I got in trouble from her." One of the girls said, almost bragging.

"No, actually, she apologized to me," I said.

"Not fair. Are you her favorite?" she questioned, in a sarcastic voice.

"I do not believe that she has favorites, but if she did, with your attitude, I suspect you would not be on her good list."

One boy quickly said, "I thought you were with us. Are you a traitor?"

"Absolutely not!"

"I dare you to not go home right now. We are going to the field to play baseball. If you are with us, you will come to watch us play."

"Certainly. My mother just requires me to do my chores." It was a little white lie. I will die if I get a white mark on my fingernail. You know, they say white lies is what causes those to appear.

I quickly looked over my fingernails and counted three. Three! Where did those come with? Tillie is always accusing me of telling white lies. She probably wished them on me.

Off we went to the field to watch the boys hit the ball. Of course, they did not have a bat. A plank of wood worked just fine.

It was an exciting game, the store-bought kids (the children who lived north of the railroad tracks) versus the millpond kids (the ones who lived south of the track and their parents worked for the lumber mill).

There were only two baseballs to be had, and when one of the boys from the millpond hit the ball so hard, it shatters the plank and sent the ball flying out of sight into the tall grasses.

Immediately, everyone knew to go in search of the prized baseball. The ball belonged to Timmy J's father, who was the man in charge of the equipment for the local men's baseball team. There was a large group of men who enjoyed playing baseball on Sundays. The teams from surrounding areas would travel to different towns to play each other. The keeper of the bats and balls held a very important job. If anything were lost, he would be responsible for buying new.

Timmy's father was an accountant and was a highly respected man in town. He took his work very seriously and counted the bats and balls just as if he were counting money. He did not play on the team but held an important job. He was no taller than Timmy was at age ten.

We searched and searched for the ball. Timmy ran home in tears, preparing for his mother, who was twice the size of his father, to whoop him. If I know Timmy, he will run indoors and confess, handing his mother the paddle. That is just the way Timmy did things. He hated to be in trouble.

We all agreed that the days of playing baseball were over. Saddened by the loss of the revered ball, we all began our somber way home.

Cecelia, my friend, and I decided to check once more in the direction of the ball.

We found it, hidden amongst the tall grass and behind a small branch. The ball, being rather old and dirty, camouflaged itself perfectly.

Holding the ball above our heads and yelling for the others, we were surprised to find that all had gone home.

"What do you think it feels like, Cecelia, to throw the ball as hard as you can? Have you ever thrown a baseball?"

"No, have you?"

"No, but I sure do have a desire right now to throw it as hard and fast as I can."

"Stand back over there and let me practice. You try to catch it."

"Don't throw it too hard, Lizzie. Remember, I do not have a glove on my hand."

Reaching down into my coat pocket, I found a regular glove and told her to put it on her hand. It would help some if the ball stung her hand when and if she caught it. I had my doubts, just knowing my friend.

I took off my coat and began mimicking the boys when they ready themselves to pitch a ball. My arm going through the motions of throwing without having a ball in my hand.

I was nearly ready when off in the distance, I heard my mother's distinct whistle for me to be home. I was distracted.

"Why could she not have waited just a few more minutes?" I asked myself.

I looked down at the ball in my hand, and I knew I had one chance to throw the ball. Again, the whistle stung the air. I hesitated. My conscience knew that I should give up on my plan and head for home. Mama would be mad as a hornet.

Then something came over me, and I wound my arm around as fast as I could. Releasing the ball into flight.

It was as if the ball were in slow motion but flying through the air with intensity as if it were on a course. I watched the beautiful ball in flight. In sudden terror, I realized that the ball was headed directly for a window.

The noise of the ball hitting the glass echoed in my head. No one else but I was responsible for the window. Looking around, Cecelia and I saw no one. It was our one chance to high tail it for home without getting caught. We took our leave, rapidly running as fast as we could.

Cecelia had to go in a different direction than I. I knew that she would be safe. As for me, I would not be in the clear until I rounded the corner at the street with the house with the broken window. My heart raced. My mother's whistle crooned through the air, followed by another and yet another. I could hear her frustration with me. I was now more focused on calming my mother down than the broken window. I would be in the clear with that erroneous error.

Do I accept my punishment for being home late, or do I try to weasel my way out of penance? I could always confess at church for disobeying my mother. My father passed away a few years prior, so it is just my mama. Do you say less hail Mary's if there is just one parent, opposed to two? Surely, you say fewer. I will beg the Priest for less.

I am almost in the clear.

As I rounded the corner, I practically bumped right into a woman standing in the way. Quickly, I excused myself, although I do not know why. It seemed as if it was neither person's fault, for you do not have eyes that can see around corners.

I began to hurriedly walk on towards home.

The woman said in a stern voice, "What is your name?"

"Lizzie, ma'am."

"Your surname dear, the name of your family, not your given name."

"Hoffman. My mother is Mary Josephine Hoffman."

"The name of your father, dear?"

"The name of my father would mean nothing to you, as he passed a few years back."

"So, your mother is a widow?"

"Yes, ma'am."

"As am I. So, I can understand and have personal knowledge of how difficult it is to raise children alone these days."

"Excuse me, ma'am, but I must go. My mother is calling for me to come home."

"Perhaps, you should have been a little more concerned about that when you threw a baseball at my window."

"Me? I beg your pardon, I do confess to being in attendance at the boys' game, but as you surely saw, there were no girls playing. It is strictly a male's game."

"My dear, do you think me blind? I was removing the last of my laundry from the line when I heard the sound of something whizzing past me. Then the shattering of glass in my upstairs window caused me to go into a panic. I did have my sense about me to look over the fence and see only two girls in the field. One of those girls being you. Since you had obviously removed your coat, you would be the obvious suspect."

"Oh no, you are mistaken. We heard the ball break your window, just as you did. We are girls and cannot throw a ball like a man. Why, if I threw that ball, it would barely drift through the air, descending right in front of me,"

"Go home, don't make your poor mother worry any longer. I shall meet her one of these days, and I will be discussing this matter with her. You will owe me for a pane of glass."

I turned and left the woman standing at the corner. A hearty round of whistles could be heard all through town. The closer I got; I could hear my name being called.

Tillie caught up to me first, warning me that mama was mad. She began questioning me profusely about my whereabouts. Scolding me as if she were my mother.

I had decided to tell mama the truth about being at the game and the boy's losing the baseball.

"Those boys were so upset over the fact that the ball belonged to the Men's team. We just wanted to help them look for it. You have taught us to help others, and that is what I was doing. I did not intend on staying out after curfew."

"Get on with your chores before dark. I will decide what to do about your absence of telling time and obligations later."

I knew mama was worried about me when I heard her tell Tillie that she was just glad I was safe.

About a week had gone by since the broken window incident. I knew I had convinced the woman that I was not the perpetrator. Out of sight, out of mind.

I raced straight home from school every day since the incident.

As I opened the back door, I realized that mama had a visitor. I peeked around the corner, and my mouth almost fell to the floor. It was her, the woman whose window I had broken. Miss. Weatherford's words, reciting the Golden Rule, was all I could hear.

"Lizzie, come into the parlor. I have someone to introduce you to."

Introductions were made.

"Sit down, Lizzie. Mrs. Renfro says she met you last week. Do you remember, Lizzie?"

"Of course, I told you mama that I was helping the boy's look for the lost ball. That was the day that I was late getting home."

"You failed to tell me that her upstairs window was broken by a baseball and that she suspects that you were the one who threw the ball. Someone has to pay for a pane of glass."

"May I remind you, Lizzie, I looked over my back fence and saw only you and another girl in the field. The baseball did not come flying into my window from the heavens. I will remind you that it is imperative you admit what you did."

I sat pondering my dilemma for what seemed a long time. I realized I had no option but to confess. My lie had caused me much anguish. I woke up one night in a panic, knowing mama would disapprove. I could not continue with my mistake.

"I did it. I was tempted when we found the ball. I held it in my hand, and I knew I wanted to experience what it felt like to pitch a ball as hard as I could throw. Obviously, I expected it to lop to the ground in front of me, as I had described to you that day, Mrs. Renfro. I surprised myself, and then I heard a pane of glass shatter. Fear came over me from what I had done. I have seen a few boys able to pitch a ball that hard."

"Indeed, you did. However, boy or girl, you must pay for the damage you have done." Mrs. Renfro said, looking over at mama.

"Lizzie, I am ashamed that you did not choose to tell the truth immediately. I think Mrs. Renfro will agree that we have all been in a situation of our own choosing that goes bad. However, I hope you have learned a good lesson from this mistake. Always tell the truth. Hard as it may be, the truth is always the best. Not only have you a windowpane to pay for, you now have to work hard to earn back my trust. That will be the hardest one."

"I am sorry, Mama and Mrs. Renfro. I will pay for the window and earn back your trust."

"Have you any money, Lizzie?"

"No, only a small amount of change."

"Then you will make the payment by doing some work for me. Being alone and a woman, I can use the help. Can you paint a fence?"

"I suppose I can learn."

"Then come over on Saturday dressed in old clothes."

"Thank you, and again I am sorry for lying to you. One more thing, may I have the baseball back to return to the team?"

"Certainly, I have no need for a baseball."

I walked out of the room, and I overheard Mrs. Renfro tell mama that she bet the baseball team would love to have a pitcher half as strong as me. I smiled to myself.

The fence got painted on Saturday with the help of Cecelia and the boys from the team.

Timmy was relieved to get the baseball back and give it to his father.

We all learned a great lesson on the truth. I want people to always tell me the truth, and I need to always tell the truth. There is something to be said for that Golden Rule.

Dear LJ,

Growing up is hard. We have to make decisions every day, and sometimes we mess up. But that is okay. That is why it is called growing up. I am going to try to think about the choices I make and work hard at following the Golden Rule. It is not new; it has been around for almost as long a man. I will strive to be the best that I can be.

McCARTY'S STATION, NEW MEXICO
PICTURE IS PROPERTY OF JK HOFFMAN

CHAPTER 17

New Friends in Old Places

Flagstaff, Arizona Territory to Fort Wingate, New Mexico Territory~1889
Age~12

I was perplexed this morning when mama called us into the parlor and said she had an important matter to discuss with Tillie and me. Odd, since she has never done that before; however, I will say that since daddy died, I no longer know what normal is around here.

Tillie and I sat quietly on the settee as mama explained that she needed to return to New Mexico for a couple of weeks. In past times, we have both stayed behind. She said that she would be taking me. Tillie will stay behind with the neighbor, Mrs. Miller. I lingered with my mouth open, not comprehending the fact that I was to accompany her.

"Close your mouth, Lizzie. You know that it is not polite or lady-like to have your mouth open for some time."

"I am sorry, Mama."

My mind was filled with crazy notions. Tillie does not enjoy caretaking the animals the way that I do. After all, most of the animals are mine. Why do I have to go with her?

I started to protest when Tillie said that she would be fine with Mrs. Miller. So that means that I shall go with Mama.

I ponder that thought in my head. I have never traveled alone with it being just mama and me. She will have to give me all of her attention. In a family our size, someone is always in need of her attention. Uh-oh, I think to myself. I will have to behave at all times. Will I get to have any fun? I hope I get to visit my friends whom I have left behind. I shall have to bide my time to see what happens.

The day arrives when we begin our journey east. Tillie is having second thoughts about being alone. Mama sits her down and explains that she trusts her to be fine. We will be just a telegraph away should she need anything.

We board the train. I, of course, choose the window seat. Mama says that she does not care about the window seat. The train is full of people ranging in age and dress. Most of the men are cowboys, but there are some men dressed in suits. All the women, including us, are dressed in our Sunday best clothes.

I mimic mama, and whatever she does, I do too... When we eat our lunch, and mama lays her napkin out on her lap, I copy her exactly. I feel a need to make a good impression on her.

It is not my place to question her about the itinerary of the trip, I subsequently relax. I do not have to think about being in control of the situation, something that I am not in the habit of doing. Just along for the trip.

I must have fallen asleep because I awaken to mama telling me that we will be getting off at the next stop. I look out the window and recognize the land east of Gallup.

Mama tells me that we are getting off at the next stop. The next stop? The stop is Fort Wingate. Why on earth would we be getting off there?

Mama explains that we are stopping over at the garrison for a couple of days for her to visit a friend. The lady and her family were old acquaintances in Michigan. She went on to say that she recently had a letter posted by her friend. Her husband is in the Calvary and has been placed at Fort Wingate. Mama promised that we would stop for a visit on our trip.

We disembarked the train to find a fine carriage awaiting us. The finely dressed Calvary men help us aboard and load our satchels. I felt like a dignitary! Tillie is missing all of this!

Looking around, there were the familiar railroad tracks, water tower, and station house. The house is two stories; similar to the ones I have seen in the past. There is usually a house upstairs where the agent lives alongside their families. It was like most train stations out in the middle of nowhere, rather desolate.

The carriage ride takes us south behind beautiful hills. I accidentally called them mountains, and mama quickly corrected me that ours are mountains, and these are hills. The hills were covered with spring flowers. It was only then that I realized how much I missed the desert flowers.

We entered the fort through an iron gate that says, "Fort Wingate, Cavalry." We stop outside a well-kept, pristine home with a white picket fence surrounding the neatly manicured lawn, including flowers and roses. It certainly was different from anything I ever saw New Mexico, much less in my life. There were other smaller homes around, but none as nice as this one.

Mama whispered to me that her friend's husband is the Commander. I had no idea that mama was friends with such important people.

We were met by the Commander and his family. Introductions were made. At mama's lead, I put my hand out to be shaken.

The family's name is Hathaway. Commander Hathaway introduced his wife Jane and his daughter, Arletta.

Arletta quickly looked at me and said, "You may call me Lettie. My real name is Arletta Cecilia Celestia Hathaway, and I am eleven years old. I am the baby of the family and the only girl. People say that I am spoiled rotten, and that is fine with me."

A chuckle went around, and I watched the Commander as he smiled proudly at his daughter. I had a twinge of jealousy, missing my own father.

Before I could delve too deeply into self-pity, Lettie burst out and announced that she would be showing me around. I was caught off guard by her telling her parents what she would do and not properly asking for permission or excusing herself. I am not a saint by any means, but her behavior surprised me.

She immediately asked me if I was an only child. I was tempted by the devil, sitting on my shoulder, to lie and say yes. How would she know? Oh, mama would discuss family with her mother. I curtly answered, saying no, expecting the discussion to end.

Wrong! She did not drop the subject. Instantly, she started in on me.

"Spill the beans. How many brothers and sisters? I want to know."

"Five," I whispered.

"So, there are six of you! Holy mother of Jesus! Your parents were like rabbits."

"Your parents let you say that? To talk about Jesus' mother like that?"

"You are a prude. I am not actually cursing or belittling his mother. However, don't go blabbing your mouth to my mother. My dad doesn't care. The soldiers all curse. They say the Lord's name in vain. I don't even think about it; unless, of course, my mother is present. You haven't said how many are males and how many are females."

I felt an urge to utter "Rabbits?" Then I caught myself. I think to myself that the girl has not shut her mouth long enough for me to get a word in edgewise.

"There are seven of us, including my mother. I have three brothers and two sisters."

"Gee, willikers! That is a crowd. I have two half-brothers, much older than me. Mama says that I am just like an only child. Does it show? I am a blue-blooded American. My family came over on the Mayflower. How about you, are you blue-blooded?"

"My parents came over on a ship from Germany in 1852."

"Then you aren't blue-blooded."

"No, my blood is red. I bleed red blood."

"Now, you are impertinent. Teasing me. I don't like to be teased."

"Then you would not get along well in my family. We tease everyone."

She then rambled on and on. I cannot get a word in edgewise. We continued to walk up the nearby hill. I just walked and listened. She pointed off in a westerly direction and told me that tomorrow, she had planned an outing of horseback riding for the two of us. I could tell by the way she spoke to me; she was expecting me to protest. I, in turn, said nothing. I was playing along with her, not letting her know if I knew how to ride or not.

We arrived back at her house near dark. I was surprised to learn that she and I would be taking dinner in the kitchen. Apparently, this was something she was quite used to doing. We walked through the maid's quarters to a back stairway up to her room. I got a glimpse of the formal dining room. I was in awe of the grandeur of the place settings. They must be expecting more guests than just mama. I giggled in my head when I thought it large enough for the whole Army. Ha! Ha!

We stayed up in her bedroom all evening, playing 'Old Maid' on her bed. It was the most comfortable bed I had ever seen. She called it a canopy bed. It had a frame over the top of the bed with a sateen covering. I, not wanting to show my ignorance, played along with her as she was describing ordering it from a catalog. She told me that it was shipped from Chicago.

As I yawned, I realized no one had been in to tell us to go to bed. Mind you, not that I cannot put myself to bed, I can. I am just so used to my mother coming in, kissing us, and saying good night. Where was mama?

"My mother did not come to tell me good-night," I said out loud.

"I do not need for my mother to tell me good-night. I am perfectly capable of going to sleep without the usual rigamarole of such pettiness."

"So am I, of course. My sister Tillie insists upon it before bed." Since she will not see Tillie, I can blame everything on her. "Where am I to sleep?"

"Come on, and I will show you to your room."

I followed her down a candlelit hallway to a guest room. In it was two beds. A larger one in the middle of the room and a smaller bed in the corner. I spotted my mother and my baggage in the small dressing area.

"Thank you, Lettie. I have everything I need. See you in the morning."

"Yes, we have a big adventure planned for tomorrow. Sleep tight and watch out for the bed bugs." She giggled as she went out of the room.

I awoke to mama dressing. I was surprised she had not tried to awaken me.

"Good morning, dear," Mama said in a cheery mood. "I slept wonderfully, how about you?"

"Yes. I did sleep well. I did not even hear you come to bed."

"It was late. Mrs. Hathaway and I stayed up visiting until all hours of the night. We had so much to get caught up on from the past. I understand the two of you girls are going out horseback riding today. I am going into Gallup to attend a luncheon with Mrs. Hathaway. You girls have fun."

Was this my mother? She did not act her usual self. Rather giddy. Almost as if she had turned into a younger version of herself.

Mama left, and I proceeded to glance around the room. I saw a riding outfit set out for me to wear. It must be Lettie's. As I examined it more closely, I spotted a tag left on it from a store. It is new. What kind of a ride are we going on that I need a new riding habit? The skirt was mid-calf, which suited me fine and dandy. The hat came with a long sash flowing down the back. The shirt was snug-fitting, with a sassy brown vest. I dressed and admired myself in the long mirror hanging behind the door.

I went downstairs into the kitchen and found the cook making a basket for our lunch. Mama and Mrs. Hathaway had already departed for the day.

Lettie appeared, ready to begin our journey. We were off to the stables.

A soldier met us and escorted us to the corrals. I had never seen so many horses in one place in my life.

I was able to choose my own horse. Of course, Lettie put in her two cents about each one I looked at to pick. The young soldier was very nice. I chose a brown gelding. The horses were experienced with riders. He saddled them up while we waited. I could get spoiled like Lettie, also. At home, when you want to ride, you saddle the horse yourself.

Lettie asked (or told, to be specific) a young officer to get two rifles for us. He obeyed her orders as if he was used to doing as he was told.

We took off in a northerly direction, stopping only at the train tracks to look in each direction for an oncoming train.

I was watching for recognizable landmarks. Johnny taught me that at our ranch. In case something should happen and you become lost, you can look for them on your return. I assumed that Lettie knew her way along the animal trails; however, I did not.

We went along the base of the limestone cliffs. We were headed east towards the morning sun. I was also taught to follow the direction of the sun for guidance and telling time.

We stopped as we came to an area that I could tell she had been at many times. It was, obviously, a place where she would shoot rifles. There were cans and bottles on the ground in a rather neat pile nearby. It became apparent to me that the soldiers used this locale for target practice.

"You do know how to shoot, don't you?" Lettie said with a snide inflection in her voice.

"A little. Enough to get by. You go first, and I will watch you. Maybe you can teach me a few tricks.

She wasted no time in loading the rifle with shells. On her instruction, she barked an order at me to set up a variety of cans and bottles. I foolishly obeyed.

To my consternation, as I was turned picking up the bottle that fell from the ledge, she shot the rifle at a target. I was livid. Obscenities started flowing from my mouth at her. The disdain I had for her at that moment overtook my normal complacency. She understood that I was about to pop a cork with her.

She immediately came at me with fists swinging. Apparently, I was supposed to have stood there and laughed at her antics. There was much hair pulling and nail scratching between the two of us.

I got away from her, and I quickly went over to the horse, untied it from the tree, and began riding back to the fort. Is all I could think of was how was I going to tell mama what happened. They would all blame me for the actions that we both took. I doubted her ability to stand up and admit to her wrongdoing. It was just not in her nature.

From behind me, she came galloping past me as if she were in a race to reach her father before I did. Noticing the rocky ravine beside me, I decided I should take it slow. I thought of Johnny and his horse going off the side of Canyon Diablo a while back. I might not be so lucky. Not that this ravine was nearly as deep a gorge as that.

I heard a horse whinny followed by a scream up ahead. Instantly, I knew Lettie was in trouble. I rode up ahead to only see the horse go running off down the trail…no rider. As I came closer, I could see her satchel on the ground, and the dirt had been badly roughed up. I heard a low whining coming from the ravine. As I began to dismount, my horse began bucking. Rattlesnakes! More than I could count, coming up and over the side of the chasm. Immediately, I pulled the rifle from its holster and began shooting at them one by one.

The repulsiveness of the blood and guts of the vermin surrounded me. Then I heard her scream. As I looked over the chasm wall, I took rapid aim at the serpent that was about to strike Lettie. I aimed the rifle and shot. Bullseye. The gory remains of the rattler spewed about, covering her with its remains. I have never witnessed anyone pick themselves up and over the side of a cliff before. She was on the back of my horse before I knew what was happening.

"Hurry, ride fast; there are more down there." Lettie was screaming at me. We rode down a piece until I spotted a shade tree.

"Why are we stopping?" She shrieked at me.

"It's alright now, Lettie. I will check the area for snakes before you get down. Just stay put while I check the ground." I immediately took my riding crop and began beating the bushes. All was clear.

"Okay, you may get off the horse now."

"Why, shouldn't we just go home."

"No, I need to know if you are injured. We also need to talk about what happened back at the beginning. Why on earth did you shoot the bottle with me standing just a short distance away?"

"I am sorry. I thought it would be a funny prank on you. I thought you were some knit-wit, scaredy-cat, girl. You sure proved me wrong. Where did you learn all of your shooting skills?"

"If you would have ever stopped talking about yourself for a minute and ask questions about me, I would have told you. You assume that because I live in a town, I have no knowledge of outdoor skills. If you had asked, I would have told you that I was raised on a ranch not far from here. My brothers taught me to shoot and protect myself. If I had not come along, you would have been down in that gulley for who knows how long."

"Thank you, Lizzie. I apologize. You must think of me as a spoiled rotten young woman. I owe you my life. Forgive me? What do we tell our parents? Mine will be most unhappy with me."

"My mama, also. In fact, that was what I was thinking about when I heard your horse whiney."

"Would it be wrong if we just told them about the snakes and not my antics with the rifle.?"

"No, I was thinking the same thing. Maybe, we could go back and start all over if you are feeling well enough. Besides, I am hungry. Should we eat our lunch here?"

"Yes, I am hungry, but not for fried rattlesnake!"

We both laughed and talked to each other normally. Then we proceeded to go back and practice our sharpshooting skills. Lettie even asked me to show her some of my tricks.

We went home friends, which made the day worth its while.

When we arrived back at the fort, the men were just starting out to look for us. When the horse appeared back without us, they began to worry. We explained to all what had happened with the rattlesnakes.

"I owe you my gratitude, Miss Lizzie, for keeping my daughter from harm's way."

Shyly, I said thank you. I explained that I was just doing what I had been taught. We boarded the train headed East the following day. Goodbyes were heartfelt, and Lettie and I promised to write often to each other. We were both happy to have made new friends.

Nellie was anxiously awaiting our arrival. We were there to help her pack her house for the move to Flagstaff.

Journal entry,

Oh LJ, I wish you could meet my new friend Lettie. It is odd when you think of it. Mama and her mother were friends in Monroe when they were both young, and now she and I are friends. I think Tillie was envious of our trip. Mama promised to travel with her one day. I learned a great lesson from my new friend; always be yourself.

Don't use a facade to fool people, or it will come back to bite you (you know, like the rattlesnakes! Ha Ha.).

Making new friends, no matter how you meet, is one of life's special gifts.

CHAPTER 18

Nellie Moves to Flagstaff

McCarty's Station, New Mexico Territory~1889 Age 12

The train pulled into the station at dusk. Stepping off the train, my mind went back to a time when life was good. My father was alive. We were a family together. A sadness shrouded me.

The air was hot. No hotter than it had been at Fort Wingate, but I felt stifled. Looking over at my mother, I felt that she was feeling the same way. Perhaps it was that we were both hoping to be greeted by him. The reality that he was gone made everything feel different.

Looking around for my sister, the town looked smaller. It was a small town, but it appeared as if it had shrunk. I know that when I lived here; the buildings did not look that tiny and insignificant.

I could see my sister, little Georgie, and William walking towards us. As they got closer, I could see that my sister was walking funny. She had a fat belly. I was older now and did not have a memory of her being with child. I could not help but giggle at her. Mama scolded me immediately.

"Mind your manners. Your sister cannot help the way she walks."

"Then you see it, also. It is not my imagination."

"Now, you are impertinent."

Lucky for me, Georgie came running up to us.

"My, how you have grown since we last saw you. You are growing tall."

"Yes, daddy says, I am his big little man. I am going to be a cowboy. I am learning to ride a horse."

"I love to ride horses. Maybe we can ride together." I said.

"Do we have horses at our new house in Flagstaff? Mama says we are going to have so much fun. Do I get my own room?"

"Georgie," Nellie scolded him. You ask too many questions and don't give people time to answer."

"You remind me so much of my George when he was your age. You are inquisitive, and that is good. You learn by asking questions." Mama told him.

"If you are my grandmother, where is my grandfather?"

"He went to heaven. He was sick here on earth, but in heaven, he is well. We miss him very much."

"The nuns talk about heaven every day. If you are bad, you can't get inside the pearly gates. What is a pearly gate? Do we have one here? I would like to see one. Do you think grandfather is inside? I hope so. If he had to wait outside for God to decide if he was good or bad, that would be awful."

Georgie did not stop talking all evening.

Georgie's father, William, worked for the railroad. He was the station agent here in McCarty's. He had put in for a transfer to Flagstaff, hoping to be a station agent there. Nellie wanted to be close to family for help with baby number two.

When the transfer came in, it was for a yardman. It would be more physical work and less pay. The decision was hard for him. He liked his job here. For the sake of the family, he would sacrifice his happiness for theirs.

We were there to help pack their belongings. I looked around and did not see much to pack. When I asked mama about it, she said that we were here to support Nellie and keep her company. We would help with what she needed.

Mama had a house built right next door to ours for the growing family. We would be right there to help with the baby. Tillie was excited about the idea of a baby to take care of for Nellie. I would volunteer to help occupy Georgie's time.

Word quickly got around town that we were here. It was difficult to work because everyone wanted to hear about our life in Flagstaff. However, we did not cook one meal. We were either brought food or invited to the homes of friends.

Mama was enjoying her time away from the stove.

William came home with a telegraph for mama. Telegraphs are so handy. You can reach someone far away, or in this case, someone down the road. The telegraph was from my new friend, Lettie's mother. She had an idea. Lettie missed me. Perhaps I could come to Fort Wingate, a couple of days, earlier and visit on my way home. The rest could come when they were ready.

"Please, mama. I would love to spend a little more time with her."

Nellie spoke up and said, "I thought you two did not get along?"

Not first, but then we decided that we liked each other. We just had to work out our differences. Lettie has grown up bossing everyone around her whole life. Until I came around. She could not boss me."

"Why does that not surprise me?" Nellie laughed.

Mama did not give me an answer right away. She was worried about me traveling on the train alone.

William explained to her that children ride on the train alone all the time. Chances are there would be another child I could sit beside.

I was on pins and needles waiting to hear if I had mama's permission. I grew more restless after I overheard mama tell William to send Mrs. Hathaway a telegram.

The reply came back quickly, yes. I jumped for joy when mama told me. Georgie was sad that I would be leaving, but we explained to him that it was just for a couple of days and that he would come to where I was staying.

I readied myself with my belongings. I said my goodbyes to old friends in McCarty's Station, knowing that I would probably never see them again.

As the train arrived, I felt important by embarking the train by myself. I found a window seat, which I have to have, and sat down. I opened the window, stuck my head out, and yelled goodbye.

The train ride was short. However, we had to stop a couple of times to wait on who knows what. They never tell you.

The conductor, the man who rides the train, takes the tickets and oversees your train car, and tells you when your stop is, knew William. He promised him that he would keep an eye on me. I still do not know what on earth they thought I would do besides sit and look out the window. Parents sometimes worry so much.

The train was rather dull and boring, and I was in a hurry to get to Lettie's. I was anxious to continue getting to know one another. We had cleared the air on what to expect from each other.

Sooner than expected, the conductor walked down the aisle announcing the arrival of the train at Fort Wingate. I grabbed my bag immediately and stood up. I quickly realized that I should not have done that; the train buckled a bit as it came to a stop, and I went forward. I was able to grab the back of the seat to hold. Then the train buckled again. This time, I forcefully sat down on the lap of a cowboy sitting in the seat.

"Oh my, excuse me, sir. I am so sorry. Forgive me." I said, feeling very embarrassed.

"Forgive me for not helping you while you were in distress, little lady."

I was thankful that the man was polite. I did not want a scene. I quickly hurried off the train.

There, waiting for my arrival, was Lettie. I was taken back a bit when she appeared to be alone. Our family is large, and we make a crowd. Seeing one person waiting for me was a surprise

We said hello, and she anxiously told me that she had a horse waiting for me.

"I hope you don't mind? I am so looking forward to riding again. I know it has only been a fortnight since we saw one another. I have missed you." Lettie confessed.

"I missed you too." I was surprised to see two horses tied to the hitching post. "Which one shall I ride?"

"The black one. It is an excellent horse."

I stopped for a moment and thought, black horse and the omen from the girl at the Loretto school? Silly me. It was just a girl I don't even know. Are you superstitious? No.

"Is anything the matter?" she questioned. "I can let you ride my horse if you would rather?"

"No, I had just thought of something from the past. It is silly. Please, ride your horse. I will be fine."

"Now, I am curious. You have to tell me." She stopped and said, "I mean, I would love to hear your story if ever you want to tell me. I will be a good listener."

Poor Lettie, her parents must be helping her choose her words before she speaks. In the past, she would have demanded and not given you a chance.

"Let me think about it. It is kind of silly. I have not talked to anyone besides my sister Tillie and LJ."

"I have heard of Tillie, but not LJ. Who is LJ?"

"LJ is my journal." I did not confess any more than that, nor did I tell her that I carry it with me, always.

"I have always wanted a journal. I like to write. Where do you get a journal?"

"My father made mine for me. It is special because he died a few months after giving it to me."

"Oh, you mean the last thing he ever gave you? How very nostalgic."

"I say sentimental since it was a gift from him."

We looked at each other and laughed. Lettie is so much more fun now that she is not a braggart.

We dropped off my bag at the house and said hello to everyone. They all said they were glad I could come back. Her parents reminded her to come in the kitchen door and up the backstairs since they were entertaining this evening.

"Yes, ma'am, I remember. We will be as quiet as mice."

We were out the door and back on the horses as fast as we could get on. Off we went down the trail and over the hill.

We rode for the rest of the afternoon.

We quietly went into the kitchen door. The cook had our plates of food ready for us. Lettie asked the cook if we could please take our food upstairs. I was surprised when she agreed.

"I will be up for your utensils in half an hour. Don't dilly-dally around."

I giggled as we went up the stairs with our plate of food. This was a rare treat for me. I had never even considered eating in my room; unless I was sick or something.

"Do you giggle at everything?"

"Yes, I guess I do." I hadn't thought about that before either.

"I could nickname you giggles."

"I like that."

We had the evening to ourselves.

The next morning, Lettie asked her mother for a journal. Her mother said she would look when she went into town.

I pondered that for a time. It must be nice to ask for something and not be told no immediately.

We left on horseback with a lunch packed from the cook. We took two rifles and a few bottles that she had collected.

She wanted to show me what she had been practicing.

Much to my surprise, she had improved so much.

The day was over before we knew it. Tomorrow would bring my family and I would be leaving.

When we arrived at the house, there was a package for Lettie; tied in brown paper with a string on it. It was a journal. Her mother wasted no time in getting her what she asked for.

"I feel rather spoiled," Lettie said as she opened the package. "You have opened my eyes to how deplorable I can act. I am ashamed of myself."

"You should not feel that way. Your parents have the means and the desire to provide you with what you want. You can now decide what is important to you and what can wait. I feel it is in your hands to decide how you are treated, just by acting and speaking differently."

"Yes, now let's go upstairs. I want to write that in my journal, lest I forget."

I got my journal out of my bag. I made it clear that she could not read it; it was my special book, just as hers would be. I did show her the leather outside, and she was very impressed it had my initials on it.

"EMH, what does that stand for?" she asked.

"My name, Elisabeth Mae Hoffman."

"Then you are like me; we both use a nickname. I am Lettie for Leticia, and you are Lizzie for Elisabeth. What is Tillie's name?"

"Mathilda," I answered. "We call everyone by their nickname except George."

We sat with our journal's open, writing until we could not hold our eyes open.

The next morning, Mrs. Hathaway said that when she walked in to check on us, we were both holding our journals, and we looked like twins.

We giggled until we could not breathe.

Lettie said, "I have to name my journal."

"Mine is LJ, for Lizzie's journal."

"If I used my initials, it would be the same as yours, LJ, for Lettie's journal."

"We would be twins again."

"Would you mind? I wouldn't use it without your permission."

"I think that would be wonderful.

"It is nice to see you become such good friends like your mama and me," said Mrs. Hathaway.

Just then, a nicely dressed soldier came in and said that the carriage was ready to go to the train station.

We rushed out the door to pick up mama and Nellie's family.

Mama was excited to introduce more of her family to her friend.

We all stayed the night and left the next day for home. I would take my memories with, me; written down safely and securely on the pages of LJ.

Dear LJ,

Didn't we have fun on our trip? I am so happy that Lettie's mama bought her a journal.

Now, she has a friend with her always. Goodnight.

Sharing common ideals and things can be fun. Remember to be respectful of others.

CHAPTER 19

Letter From Lettie

Fort Wingate, New Mexico Territory
Age 13

MY DEAREST LIZZIE,

I have been thinking of you and wishing you were here with me. Life out here seems so lonely without you. I think back to your visit and wish that I had not been so high and mighty when you first arrived. I frittered away our precious time together.

When you first arrived, I was a mere girl. As my daddy says, spoiled and overindulged. He blames it on my dear mother.

I say it is he, as much or more than her. I feel there are times when I am but a nuisance to him. It comes easier for him to distract me with trivial and useless gifts.

You opened my eyes to a happier me. I was able to see things differently. I had never thought of myself as unhappy, but alas, I was most miserable with myself.

I did not care about who or what I hurt. I was only looking out for myself. Apparently, I was getting enjoyment out of making others miserable around me.

After you were gone, I felt so alone and miserable myself. I was angry at everyone. I acted as an impudent child. I deserved the same behavior that I gave to others. Especially to you. In turn, that did not happen.

My mother confessed to me that she and your mother had a long discussion on the train. Mother cried on her friend's shoulder, confessing that she did not know what she would do with me. Mother confessed that she was envious of your mother for raising a daughter like you. Your mother is kind and patient with you.

Your mother offered advice: to be firm, follow through with punishment, let your children make mistakes (apparently, we learn better if we trip and fall a few times), and give the same love and respect to all your children.

My mother came home and had a long talk with my father. They agreed to do things differently.

I had always been immediately sent to my room and never heard anything else about my behavior. What kind of punishment is that?

I was perplexed when I was asked to sit in the parlor to discuss my behavior. We all agreed it was not acceptable.

Then my mother asked me how I thought I should be reprimanded. Can you imagine; me deciding how I should be punished?

Of course, my first thought was to answer back with a snide remark. I stopped myself and imagined the cliff that I had gone over when you were visiting. I pictured myself balancing on the edge of that cliff right then. Would I make the same mistake and go over the cliff, or would I stop and turn around?

I pictured you being there for me and suddenly realized that instead of you, my parents were sitting there for me. They were patiently waiting for me to decide my own future. I truly wanted and needed their guidance, love, and understanding.

I had an epiphany; I wanted my life to change for a happier, calmer attitude. I wanted people to like and respect me.

I did not want to be the know-it-all bully with a chip on my shoulder. I would change for me, knowing that I have to live with myself for the rest of my life with no regrets. Do you think it is possible to change overnight?

Look at me, rambling on. I have been rude not to ask about yourself and your family. Are you well?

Did you enjoy your trip? Did Nellie get moved to Flagstaff?

I have so many questions.

Mother and I are planning a trip to Chicago in a few weeks to visit family. Mother says that if I wish, I can stay back there and broaden my horizons. Whatever that means. We are so encapsulated here at the fort; I am not exposed to the world as she thinks I should be.

She is thinking of my future and that no respectable man would want to marry a girl who had grown up isolated in the New Mexico Territory. My mother has high hopes for me. A soldier would be fine with me. Picture me at a lavish dinner party telling of coyotes and a good rattlesnake cooked over an open flame. I can see the ladies running out of the room with their hankies covering their mouths, as not to vomit in public.

While I expound on the delicacies of the white meat cooked on a stick, with the coyotes singing in the background. A perfect evening.

I shall not keep you any longer, my dear friend. I am anxiously awaiting your reply.

Sincerely yours,
Lettie Hathaway

Dear LJ,

I received a letter today from my dear friend Lettie Hathaway. Imagine how I felt walking into the post office and asking for our mail. I was handed my very own letter. It was my first letter. I proudly held it up for all to see.

At first, I thought of our relationship as a lost cause. I could not picture us as friends. I have no tolerance for bullies and know-it-alls. I judged her as she had judged me. We were both wrong. It is a shame that we live so far apart from each other. At least we can stay in touch with letters.

Who are we to judge others?

CHOCOLATE FALLS~GRAND FALLS, LEUPP, ARIZONA
NAVAJO RESERVATION
PICTURE PROPERTY OF JK HOFFMAN

CHAPTER 20

The Chocolate Falls

Flagstaff, Arizona Territory to Grand Falls, Arizona Territory~1890
Age 13

The sun is shining after several days of spring rains and snow. Mother nature cannot make up her mind if it is spring or winter.

From my bedroom window, I can see the mountain for the first time in a week or more. The snow-capped peaks make her look like a royal palace. Enchanting, yet mysterious, stunning yet elusive. I could watch her all day. The sun is so bright on her high snow-covered top, making her tallest peak appear as if it is a pyramid. The native Indian tribes believe that she is the home of the Gods. Sacred mountain, the name the Indians gave her. I feel that way also.

I can hear Mama down in the kitchen. The smell of bacon frying makes my tummy growl. I am hungry this morning. I dress quickly so that I will be ready for church.

Often on Sundays, the men come in from the ranches for a good home-cooked meal. After all, it has been some time since we have seen them. The weather keeps them away. They ride the rangelands looking for cattle that have wandered away. Every animal is worth the money. Bertie says that the foreman worries more about the cattle than the ranch hands. It is easier and cheaper to find men to replace than cattle. The owners expect to replace men but not the herd.

"Mama, are the men coming to town today?"

"I will believe it when I see them walk through that door."

Just as Mama finished speaking, the back door opened, and in walked George and Johnny.

"My, you boys are here early. What brings you to town at this time of day? You must have caught the early train from Two Guns."

"Mama," exclaimed Johnny, "We came to take you back with us.

"Back with you where?" Mama questioned.

"Out to Two Guns. We have found the most beautiful waterfall." George utters. "We actually came to invite the three of you to attend an outing with us today."

Mama relaxes a bit as George goes on to tell her about the discovery.

"Johnny was out that way, looking for stray calves when he heard water. Now, this is a high desert, and you just don't hear a waterfall out in the middle of nowhere. You know water is hard to come by. We want to share this with you, women. We have been told that it only happens in the spring after heavy snow and rain. We don't know how long it will last. The eastbound train leaves in an hour. Will you come with us?"

"Well," she stammers. Mama is not a person who does things on the spur of the moment. "I planned to go to mass, as I always do on Sunday. Not to go flaunting myself on a holy day across the plains. It would be sacrilegious. What would people say?"

George quietly explains to Mama that we must sometimes take our church out of doors and enjoy the beauty that He has created. God won't punish you for enjoying his handiwork, he explains.

Lucky for us, Mama listens to George. She turns to us and says, "Girls, go change into something more appropriate for an outdoor excursion."

It does not take a second for us to go running up the stairs and change.

Johnny just keeps saying that it looks like a chocolate fountain. I cannot wait to see it. My excitement is hard to contain. We have not had an outing for some time now.

The train arrives on time, which makes me happy. I quickly scan the car for the best seats. Of course, I want a window seat. It is not a long ride, stopping at Winona to let passengers on and off. Then we begin the ride again.

Next stop, Two Guns. Johnny and George both warn us about the town. It is said to be one of the wildest towns in this region. The sheriff's lives are short-lived here. Some lasting less than half a day before being shot and killed. It is a roughneck town.

We won't be staying long, so I am not worried. In fact, I rather hope to see some excitement. I won't tell Mama or Tillie that. They already think that my head is full of marbles.

Bertie is waiting for us as the train arrives. We get into the carriage that he has rented for the day.

We begin our journey headed north on a well-worn wagon trail. As long as Bertie stays within the ruts, the ride is not bad. However, once in a while, we get a jolt. Mama offers to drive the carriage. However, Bertie says no. George and Johnny are on horseback.

There are vast open spaces with little vegetation. A lone tree every once in a while. I watch the jackrabbits running away from us in sheer panic. We disturbed their normally serene life. The men keep saying that there is a deep canyon up ahead. I can see nothing that gives a hint of any such thing.

I ask if I may ride on the back of one of their horses, and Johnny quickly says yes. I ride in front of him, seeing all of the landscape. We are going at a rather slow pace, and suddenly he asks me if we should go faster. I quickly say yes and hold onto the reins as tight as I can, and off we go. We arrive faster to our destination than those in the buggy. I much prefer a horse to an enclosed buggy. I like to let my hair down and feel the wind in my hair.

We dismount a safe distance away from the canyon, and Johnny explains that we need to tie the horse up securely. I am anxious to see the water. We walk carefully to a pristine spot to see the waterfall. I gasped when I first saw it. It does look like chocolate! There are several small ledges above the falls that look like they have been purposely placed for the water to make its way towards the large waterfall.

As I peered over the edge, I can see a whirlpool swirling around with trapped logs and limbs, along with grasses. I am intrigued by the beauty of it.

Tillie arrives with Bertie and Mama. Tillie gasps as she watches nature in full sight. I thought she might be afraid, but instead, she is mesmerized by the canyon.

We laid out our blanket near the edge of the south side of the steep walls. Water spray lands upon us, and Mama insists that move or else we shall look as if we are covered in chocolate ourselves.

Mama brings out the lunch basket that she brought with us. Bertie has brought the blanket which Mama made for him. She took old jeans and made a quilt from them. It is nice and thick so that we don't get pricked by the undergrowth.

When we are finished with our lunch, the men proceed to take a nap. Mama brought along her knitting, as did Tillie. Me, I just sit and watch the water flow over the sides of the red canyon walls. When the wind blows, we can feel the mist coming from the falls.

Tillie complains that the muddy water will get her yarn dirty. Johnny teases her that she should have never brought it out here. This place has been here much longer and will outlast her knitting.

From the top of the canyon, it makes a hairpin curve. I venture off to follow the river north.

Off in the distance, I can see a small Navajo boy herding sheep. I wave at him, and he waves back. I envy him his freedom out in nature all day. I could herd sheep all day. Then I spotted his black and white dog.

I venture closer to the side of the canyon. I was looking for a trail that would take you down to the bottom. I would like to be down there so that I could look at it from a different direction. The trail is steep.

Johnny can almost read my mind and explains that there is an animal trail that meanders down a side cliff. He suggests that maybe one day, he can bring me back, and we will hike down to the bottom.

My mind wanders, and I imagine myself being a giant and stepping down the ledges like they are stairs. The floor of the canyon is green grass growing up beside the banks of the river. Everything is happy when there is water to be had. The birds are flying overhead, and George points out an eagle flying overhead. Hawks and other small birds were enjoying the warmth of the day.

As I peered out over the terrain, I see the boy bringing the herd of sheep closer towards us. I wave again. He motions for us to come towards him. I ask Mama if it is okay if I go to him.

"Just watch your step. There can be prairie dog holes. I don't need you getting hurt."

"Okay, Mama. I will watch my step."

I want to run towards him, but I obey. As we near each other, I see that his hair is as black as mine. His hair is wrapped in a bun tied with white yarn.

He says hello to me, and I answer back. He tells me that his name is Bahe McCabe and he is home from a boarding school in Gallup just to help with the spring shearing. I tell him my name, and we enjoy each other's company. He says it is nice to talk to someone. He gets lonely out here all day by himself. He pulls a handful of pinon nuts out of his pocket and shares them with me. I have never eaten one before, so he shows me how to crack it with my teeth. Inside the little brown shell is a white nut. I like the flavor.

"Where does this come from?" I ask.

"It is the seeds of the pinon trees." He shows me the necklace around his neck.

"That is very pretty."

"Would you like to have it? It is yours if you want it."

"Oh, I couldn't take your necklace."

"It is my gift to you. Besides, I can always make another one."

I take it from him and place it around my neck. "Thank you. I will cherish this always."

Suddenly, we are both startled as we hear the sound of a shotgun. I have never been shot at before in my life. We both fall to the ground to safeguard ourselves.

"What just happened?" I exclaimed to him. "Who shot at us?"

"Be still," he said quietly.

We look up from our safe spot on the ground to see Johnny coming towards us carrying his gun.

"Are you two okay?" Johnny asks.

"What in tarnation just happened?" I blurt out.

"Easy sister. While you two were visiting, a coyote decided to move in on your herd. I had no choice but to shoot at him. I didn't kill him; I just scared him off."

"You did not kill the Ma'ii?"

I laugh and ask, "What is a Ma'ii?"

"It means coyote in Navajo," Bahe explained. "He has power over rain."

"Is it bad that Johnny at shot him?" I ask.

"No, my father would be very angry with me if he knew that I had taken my eyes off the sheep. I am very grateful to you. The coyote is special to us in our beliefs."

Johnny explains that he had been watching the coyote come in towards the sheep.

We say our goodbyes as the family is packing up preparing to leave.

I wave back towards my new friend, saddened by the fact our meeting was so short. I wished I could return to see him again, but now, I will never see him again.

Our day at Chocolate Falls has come to an end. I am happy and sad.

The buggy ride back to the train did not seem to take as long as the ride out. I wonder why that is when you go the same amount of distance.

Dear LJ, we had such a good day today. When we said our prayers tonight, I thanked God for letting me meet my new friend. I will think about him often out there, herding his sheep. I will put the necklace in a special place, for I want to keep it forever to remind me of him. I think I shall dream of chocolate falls all night.

You never know where or who you will meet in this life. Someone can be your friend if only for a day.

SNOW PICTURE IN FLAGSTAFF, ARIZONA
PICTURE IS PROPERTY OF JK HOFFMAN

CHAPTER 21

Broken Bones Can't Hold Me Back

Flagstaff, Arizona Territory~1890
Age 14

Spring should be arriving soon, I thought to myself as the March winds and snow whirled around me. It had snowed several inches during the night and continued throughout the morning. The snow was bad enough, but the wind was unbearable as I tried to walk down the street. I tried to look out from the tightly wrapped scarf around my head and neck. My eyes were instantly filled with snowflakes. Of course, they melted as soon as they touched my face. At one point, the wind was so strong that I felt as if it were going to carry me away.

Luckily, I was getting close to home. Normally, Tillie would be with me; however, she was at home sick with a cold. Mama did not want her outdoors in this weather.

The last climb up the hill was challenging. My satchel blew out of my hands and down the hill. I had no choice but to go running after it. The wind was pushing at my back. Mama had sent me to the store for a few potatoes and onions for our stew. This late in the winter, our supplies were running low. I found the onion and potatoes strewn across the road. Four vegetables, I had five. Now, where could the last one have gotten too?

"Oh, there you are," I said to myself out loud. It was buried beneath the new-fallen snow.

Hurrying in the snow is difficult. My shoes made me slip on the wet, cold snow. I knew that Mama would be worried; I hurried even more.

One moment I was standing headed North, and the next minute I was lying on the ground, headed South. When I tried to get up, I felt a horrible pain in my wrist and then one on my ankle. I could do nothing but lie in wait for a passerby to help me get home.

Tears instantly came to my eyes. I didn't know if I was crying because of the pain or that I felt stupid. I could feel the snow covering me with snowflakes.

On a day like today, everyone who is smart is inside their homes staying warm and dry. It could be a long while before help arrives. By instinct, I began calling 'Help!'

If I could turn myself around, maybe I could scoot myself towards a bush. There were no trees. This was the first area that the loggers cleared of the old forest.

As I began pushing with my good foot and hand, I realized I was making mud with my warm body. Without thinking, [Tillie would tell you that I never think], I laid my face down in the wet, brown earth. I used my good hand to wipe my hair away from my face. Now, I was covered in the sticky clay. Mama will be angry with me when I get home.

My mind raced. What if no one found me here on the ground? I could imagine everyone crying and mama feeling bad for sending me to the market. Poor little Lizzie left out here in the cold all by herself.

Time seemed to stand still. I questioned myself, had I been here long? It was not dark yet. Perhaps there was still hope. My voice felt weak as I called once again for help.

Someone was beside me. Or could it just be my imagination? I tried to see if anyone was there. No one. Am I delirious? I have heard tales of angels coming when a person is near death. Could it have been them? Why would they come for me; Tillie says that I am so ornery, the devil wouldn't take me. I won't go with them. I shall have to tell them to find someone else today.

The cold was starting to make my toes feel numb. I must be brave. How can I be when my eyes do not stay open?

I was dancing in a field of clover, with butterflies and birds all around me. I was surprised when a monarch butterfly landed on my hand. It was so beautiful with its black, orange, and white wings. It spoke to me, saying that I followed it home. Yes, home. I must get home to mama and Tillie.

"Will you take me home? I need help; I am injured. It is my ankle and wrist."

"Yes, sweetheart, we will get you home and into a nice warm bed."

"That is funny; how will a butterfly get me home? Your voice sounds just like mama's."

"Lizzie, Lizzie, open your eyes. Look at me."

"I am looking right at you, Mr. Butterfly. I am sorry, I mean, Mrs."

There was the sound of laughing. You know that nervous giggle when people are upset. I did not know that butterflies could laugh.

"Just hold onto me while I pick you up." This time it was a deep man's voice.

I instantly said, "No, I don't want to hurt your beautiful wings, and I am much too heavy for you."

"I've got you. Trust me."

"Yes, Mr. Butterfly, I trust you," I said as I drifted off in slumber.

The candle flickered in my bedroom as I opened my eyes. I was expecting to see a Monarch standing watch over me, so I was surprised when it was my mama. She was sitting in her rocking chair, dozing. She was not a beautiful butterfly; she was my beautiful mother.

I said excitedly, "Mama, I didn't die." I thought a butterfly was taking me to see daddy in heaven."

"You are safe at home now, Lizzie. Thanks to some boys walking home after a day of snow play. They came and told me you had fallen. Of course, to hear them, you were lying dead in the road. Boys always exaggerate everything."

"But, Mama, what about the field of clover with birds and butterflies all over? It was too real. I could not have imagined that."

"Yes, Lizzie, you did imagine it in your mind. It is called delirium. I suffered from it once while I lived with my oma [grandmother in German]. Like you, I slipped and bumped my head on ice. You have a large goose egg on your forehead."

"You mean that I did not die?"

"No, Lizzie, you have a broken wrist and a sprained ankle. Dr. Brannen came and wrapped them in a splint. You will not be going anywhere until you are healed."

This is the worst thing that could happen right now. There are so many things to do as we get into Spring.

"Get some rest now, and don't spend all of your time pouting about what you can and cannot do with yourself. You can help me get caught up on the mending."

"But, Mama, I am not one to stay indoors. Especially as the weather warms. My pony will need exercise, and you need help in the garden."

"Tillie can take over all of the chores. Don't 'but Mama" me.

She then left me alone. I sat and contemplated my confinement. For some girls, laying around in bed all day is fine. I am not that type. I do have some books that I have wanted to read. I will send Tillie to the library. She will need to do as I tell her.

Two weeks have gone by, and I have managed to crawl down the stairs. I asked Dr. Brannen if I could at least try standing on my foot. He said, "Absolutely not!"

I think that tomorrow I shall try on my own. What is the worst thing that could happen? I guess I could fall. Okay, with that in mind, I shall need to steady myself. If only I could get Tillie to help, I stand on my own. Hum? I wonder how I can get her to help.

I will need a plan. I need to think of something that my sister really despises doing.

I hear a noise outside. I think that some of my friends have stopped by to visit me today. They are probably wondering what has happened to me by now.

My curiosity is getting the better of me. I have a strong desire to get out of this bed right now and walk over to the window. Better yet, if I can go downstairs, maybe I could get to the front porch where we could sit and visit.

Mama is out this afternoon, so it is just Tillie and me. Here I go. Wish me luck.

I slide off of the feather bed and onto the floor as gently as I can. Taking each stair with my bum flat against the step. Slowly and carefully, I make my way downstairs. Of course, getting up is going to be harder with my broken wrist.

I can hear them talking to Tillie. They are telling her that a group of us have been invited next week out to a barn dance east of town. She indicated that she so much wants to attend. No mention of me. Then I hear them tell her that Jesse Gregg will take his wagon for everyone to ride.

My mind starts to analyze my situation. If Tillie sees me down here, she will blab to mama. Mama will then tell me no. I turn around and carefully make my way back up the stairs, protecting my wrist from injury.

When Tillie comes up to see me, she says rather sarcastically that a group of friends came to visit.

"Oh, that was nice. What did you tell them?"

"That you were confined to bed because of your injuries."

"Is that all they wanted?"

"No, they came to tell me about a dance. Too bad that you will have to stay home. I think I shall wear my new pink dress and bonnet."

She was really trying to get under my skin. If I give in and say something rude, she will blab to mama. I think I shall just shrug my shoulders and go on with my reading.

"Lizzie, did you not listen to a word I just said?"

"I heard you. A barn dance. If I know mama, she will say that if all of us can't go, then we all must stay home."

"You little urchin. You would make me stay home and babysit you. Oh please, Lizzie, you just have to get stronger. I can help you walk. Let's practice right now, while mama is out."

"You promise you won't say a word to her about my being up?"

"I promise. Now, let's get started. Okay, stand up, and I will help you."

We practiced all the while mama was away. By the time she returned, I had made a vast improvement in my walking. I began walking around the room at a normal pace. There was no stopping me now.

"Look, Mama, my ankle is almost good as new."

"Time and rest, just as the doctor ordered, has done you good. Just don't go over using that foot today."

"Good idea, Mama. I will go rest on the settee while you and Tillie fix dinner." A scowl came my way from Tillie.

Was she hoping that I could not go on the trip? Was there someone that was going that she would rather I not know about?

It was too late for that. I already knew about her and Jesse Gregg being all smoochie. I can see a lot of things going on from this window.

I have wanted to ask her about her new beau. I know who he is, but I have never talked to him. He always stops, and they hold hands and gaze into one another's eyes longingly before he tips his hat and walks away. Maybe I am exaggerating a bit but not too much.

Tillie would just say that I am jealous. I can only picture myself with one man, and that is Ed. He is my one true love. He hardly knows I am around. Only to tease me and make other girls jealous.

The day arrived for our excursion out to the barn dance came. When mama announced that she would be attending, there was no reason that I could not go. You could see that Tillie had other ideas and was disappointed.

She asked if she could ride in the wagon with Jesse.

"I am almost fifteen, mama.

The parade of buggies was impressive. You could tell everyone needed a festive event to celebrate the end of winter.

We were all greeting friends. The band started up, and everyone took to the dance floor.

I, of course, stood against the wall with my girlfriends. Gossip was the word of the night. We would see someone, and immediately the talk would start. Tillie and Jesse came by, oblivious to us.

It seems that they were the most talked-about couple going. I learned it had been going on for some time now. Tillie had even been seen in the Episcopalian church the last few Sundays.

Apparently, while mama stayed home with me on Sunday morning, Miss Tillie had taken it upon herself to explore places of worship. In fact, the padre had suggested it to us a few months back. Leave it to Tillie to place herself as a self-appointed Ambassador of kindness.

I smiled as my friends kept talking about them.

Just as one girl started to say that she had seen them behind a tree, a group of cowboys came inside.

My eyes searched the group and Johnny was there. Was Ed here? No sign of him. Johnny would tell me.

I made the mistake of walking up to Johnny and tried to talk with him. He was in no state of mind to visit. When he asked if mama was here and I said yes, he immediately left. Apparently, he did not want to cause a scene with her. Not that mama would. She would wait until she saw him next time and give him a piece of her mind.

Ed appeared as we were about to leave. He grabbed me by the arm, and we danced. Briefly, I was blissfully happy. Until an older woman came and asked him if he was through with the children's dance lessons.

I was furious at her and was glad to be leaving.

Then he stopped again and turned around, "Are you feeling better now, Liz? I heard about your accident. Sorry I didn't make it by to visit you. Your brothers kept me posted on your recovery. See you next time, cyclone. You get better at dancing every time." He gave me a wink and blew me a kiss.

Was that it? does he think blowing me a kiss makes everything better? Does he think that he is doing me a favor by dancing with me? My dance instructor? Next time, I will show him.

He left getting a lecture from the woman on his arm.

"See you next time, cyclone. You get better at dancing every time."

That would be who knows when and for now I had some spying to do on Tillie and Mr. Gregg.

Spring and summer could be interesting.

Dear LJ,

Guess what I heard about Tillie tonight at the dance? She and Jesse are the talk of the town. Ah, spring. Love is in the air. First, I need to find out if mama knows or not. I have work to do.

Yes, I saw Ed. I am hotter than a green chili on the fire. Does he think I will melt into butter in his hand at the sight of him? I know I do. But that is our secret. Love you, LJ.

Why is it that after a long winter, does the mention of spring gives us new hope?

CHAPTER 22

A Cataclysm of the Highest Proportion

Flagstaff, Arizona Territory~1892
Age 15 Years 8 Months 10 Days

Dear LJ,

Are we judged by how many tragedies one person can endure? If so, then I must be viewed as a hardy soul.

I have now suffered the loss of both of my parents. I am at present an orphan. However, I am not completely alone. I have my five brothers and sisters. Although, it is Tillie and me who no longer have a home to return to at the end of the day.

You see, my house was lost in a great fire. With that, the fire took with it the lives of my mother and a little boy by the name of Eddy.

Looking at the ashes of our belongings opened my eyes. Lives can be lost in an instant. Life is precious. I have so many things to tell my mama. I was too busy having fun.

Ed was there for me from the moment I reached the fire. He wrapped me in a blanket and held on to me. He was consoling me and wiping my tears. When I was with him, I felt like I was not alone. Surely, he must have feelings for me? He would not be so heartless as to tease me with his affection at this dark time in my life? That would be cruel.

I cannot dwell on Ed right now. He comes in and out of my life like a ball bouncing haphazardly in a big room. It is there one minute, and without a word, it is gone. The ball is picked up by someone else; it slipped through your fingers again. Then before you know it, the ball bounces back to you.

I will admit this only to you, LJ. I feel as if I belong in his arms. It is a natural feeling of happiness. I love Ed Geddes. I want to tell the world how I feel. My fears are valid. Does he feel the same for me? Or am I still the little girl he first met years ago? Does he love her more than me? Do I risk everything by confessing my love?

I cannot bother my sisters with my menial concerns. They are much too busy at making decisions for Tillie and my well-being. Tillie is also consumed with grief and consoled by Jesse. As for my brothers, all of them unattached, single. What would they know of love?

Does he know that girl will be gone forever? Will he mourn the loss of her, or can he accept the woman I have become?

So many questions and no answers. I shall wait patiently for Ed.

I have you, my dear LJ. If only you could guide me, give advice, or even scold me like mama used to do to me. Instead, you listen quietly, letting me expound on my emotions.

You are a clever one, LJ. You force me to see the answers to my own questions there in front of me on your pages. You give me power from deep inside me. Thank you, my friend, for your constant companionship.

The days following my mother's funeral are a blur to me. We do not have a home of our own to return to for solace. I am not even wearing my personal clothes.

I hate the wind. For it is the wind that caused the fire. The kerosene lamp blew over. Eddy was asleep. Mama slipped out and went across the street to visit with Mrs. Miller. They both saw the flames. Mama ran to get Eddy out; at that moment, he was her only concern. It was too late. Her dress caught fire, erupting into flames. Both gone before help could arrive.

Jesse heard the customary three rifle shots in a row. The alarm signaling a fire. In this town, fire is our enemy. Parts of town are completely lost by fires. Everyone panics then prepare themselves to help fight the flames. The volunteer's minds are on saving lives and structures. Word spread quickly through the water lines that all was lost. Deep despair could be heard in people's voices as they shared the news with one another.

When Tillie and I appeared, a concern for us was evident. The weaker souls avoided us. I was lucky to find LJ sitting on the floor under the seat of the buggy. Exactly where I had stashed her as I exited the carriage, leaving mama and Eddy on their own. Any other night, Tillie and I would have been there. Would things have been different? No one wanting to be 'the one' who broke the news. The strong had to muster their strength from deep inside the place in all of us that we know is there but only use it in times of immense tragedy.

My first thoughts were that the onlookers were seeing us as children. They felt the need to protect us from the realities of life. I knew I had to see her. I had to know. It is who I am. Tillie was the opposite. It's neither a strength nor a weakness on both our parts. It is who we are. Do not judge or criticize either of us.

Once I saw her, I knew that my life had changed. The fun-loving, adventurous tomboy was suddenly forced to grow-up.

I had to find the strength to return to the property. I cannot call it home.

I exited the carriage, leaving mama and Eddy on their own. Any other night, Tillie and I would have been there. Would things have been different?

With the help of the townspeople, donations were many. Food was brought to the boarding house where we were staying. It helped the innkeeper keep the hordes of visitors fed.

My cow and cat were found. Mrs. Miller offered to look after them until such time we were ready to take them.

Boots, the cat, was spoiled with fresh cream daily.

The black figurine horse was never found. Gone forever, melted into a liquid from the heat of the intense fire.

Each day brought us closer to the reality that our brothers and sister would not be able to finish raising us.

Plans were being made for us to travel to Michigan to stay with an uncle. My mother's half-brother Bernard Sturn and his wife Matilda, she was my father's half-sister. Tillie was named after her.

I was anxious for an adventure. Tillie did not want to leave Jesse. With Jesse's blessing, she agreed to travel.

What would be waiting for us there? I could not wait to find out.

Dear LJ,
We are going on a journey by train to Monroe, Michigan.

As in life, when one chapter ends, another one begins.

PART THREE

FLAGSTAFF, ARIZONA
TERRITORY~1892–1895
AGES~15–18

EAST VIEW OF SAN FRANCISCO PEAKS
FLAGSTAFF, ARIZONA
PROPERTY OF JK HOFFMAN

Letter of Sympathy and Hope

Chicago, Illinois~Summer 1892
Age~15

My Dearest Lizzie,

Mother received a telegraph from father today telling her of the great tragedy of your mother's passing.

Words cannot begin to express our deepest sympathy to you and your family.

Mother and I, arm in arm, fell to the floor in tears. We cannot imagine that such horrendous events could befall such a wonderful woman.

You poor darling, how are you and your family coping? You must be beside yourself with grief.

I do know you, Lizzie, and you are a strong, remarkable, and courageous woman. Your character is awed by many. That is why I trust that you, my friend, will pull through this tragic event stronger than ever before.

Father mentioned that you may be traveling to the Midwest to stay with family in Monroe, Michigan. Mother and I now live in Chicago. The train stops here, and you would need to change trains to travel north. Please consider staying over with us for a few days, either on your trip up or back home.

Mother decided that I should be attending a more prominent school back here. The education is far superior to the schooling I received at a fort in the middle of nowhere. There I go sounding as if I am bragging again.

I plan on applying to the university to become one of the first women doctors in Chicago. My dream is to cause a change in women's lives. A small family practice serving the indigent would satisfy my ambition.

As you can probably tell, I am active in pushing for the right for women to vote in this country. I am also active in the temperance movement.

When you visit, I shall introduce you to some of the brave women involved. A woman I know was arrested and jailed for participating in the march we attended last week. It is rumored that her husband was behind her arrest. We cannot ask her for details because no one has seen or heard from her since. Some men are known to have placed their wives in asylums for disobeying them.

My question being, what in the world are those men doing, and what are they hiding from women voting or holding public office? They are obviously afraid of women. I am sure the history books will never divulge that information within its pages.

Pardon me for ranting on and on.

I do wish that I were there for you. We could saddle our horses and ride through the forest as Lady Godiva did.

Laugh, my friend, laugh, until you cry so hard you cannot cry another tear. Remember that I am here crying with you.

Please, do consider meeting up with mother and me in Chicago.

Your Fort Wingate Friend,
Lettie Hathaway

CHAPTER 24

Recovering From A Great Loss

Arizona Territory~22 May 1892
Age~15

"How does one recover from a death?"

The old Padre stood in his pulpit and began his sermon. All eyes, it seemed, to be upon me. That was how I felt.

I was sitting in our family row, alone; no one else in the family could bring themselves to attend the usual Sunday Service.

"Do not mourn for them. Mourn for yourself. For those who are gone are now with God."

I wish I could be invisible. There was no escaping now without everyone in the church seeing me. I already had to put up with "How are you coping, child?" from everyone in attendance when I walked inside the church my mother loved. She was a big part of the building of this sanctuary.

I took myself back to a time when we first arrived in Flagstaff. The town was so new that most religions did not have churches. We met in the homes of the congregation. We did not have a Priest. The Catholic Dioceses, located in Phoenix, did not feel that it was necessary to have a priest if we did not have a Chapel. Our congregation worked hard that year, raising money for the construction. Mama had been an active part of helping with the Autumn Bazaar, which we raised over eight hundred dollars. We were here, in this very chapel, by Christmas Eve. A feat that onlookers said could not be done. Although not finished, a mass was held. We would now have our very own priest.

I realized that the congregation was standing for a hymn. Just as I stood up, I could feel someone slide in next to me. My eyes were closed, and my head down. I opened one eye to see highly polished boots. It was not my brothers; their boots were worn and dirty.

It was Ed. He smelled clean as if he had just come from the bathhouse. My eyes still closed; I breathed in the familiar smell of Hood's French Cologne'; a smell I had grown accustomed to because it was popular with many men, especially one tenderfoot cowboy from Kansas. I relaxed, knowing it could only be Ed sitting next to me. He has been here for me since that awful night. Unwavering in his attention to my family and me. He never judged or preached to me during this time. He let me talk or not talk.

He was there for mama's funeral. He was there for all of us.

As we exited the church, I was bombarded with people asking me questions… he spoke for me. My face was hidden under the black lace mantilla.

We walked home [the boarding house, which was my new temporary lodgings]. On Sunday, a large noon meal was served. We entered the dining area as everyone was sitting down. I hesitated, not feeling hungry. Besides, eating with a group of mainly men you do not know was not what I was ready for yet. Ed sensed my feelings. Just before I was preparing to sit down, He said, "Liz, did you forget something? We were supposed to see Mrs. Miller after church."

Taking his lead, I said, "I am so forgetful, I forgot. Please excuse us."

We walked out the door, and he said, "I know a place where we can get some food. Don't go thinking it is all that good, but edible."

I think you could call that our first date. There was no kissing, only the support I needed.

The family went to Gregg's house. Jesse and his family welcomed the Hoffman family with open arms.

When Ed and I returned to the boarding house, I was informed that a message was left for me. I was expected to make my appearance at Jesse's.

We walked up the hill to the house. When I walked in with Ed, Johnny had been drinking, and he tried to punch Ed.

Ed left before any more trouble happened. I didn't even get to thank him for being there for me today.

I sat in a corner, embarrassed and angry at Johnny for his behavior. Mrs. Gregg came up to me and welcomed me to her home. Apparently, Mr. Gregg has had that same problem as Johnny. "Doesn't know when he's had enough," was how she worked her sentence.

Nellie had gone out after Ed. She ran him down and asked him directly as to what his intentions were with me.

I was later told that he said, "Madam, I am a family friend, which includes your youngest sister. I have a great concern for her well-being, but it is nothing more than that."

"She is at a vulnerable time in her life, and you cannot lead her on, letting her think that you are in love with her."

"When I am madam, you will be the first to know what my intentions will be. As for now, rest assured that I only have her well-being in mind."

He tipped his hat at her and left.

Upon learning this news from Tillie a few days later, answered my question as to where Ed had been.

My heart sank, and I cried myself to sleep, all alone in my room at the boarding house.

I realized that my old life was over. Unsure as to what lies ahead for me, I managed to live life on my own. I would oversee me and no one else. My brothers and sisters would need to accept that I was now going to be making my own decisions. They could offer me choices, but ultimately, the choices were mine, and mine alone.

A few days later, the family approached Tillie and me. They made arrangements that we go to stay with family in Michigan for the summer. That way, the men could get a new house built for us.

George told Ed that I was anxious to see him. Ed came calling at the boarding house, and I told him about the plan for us to travel to the Midwest.

He gave me his blessing and said that he would be here, punching cattle, until I returned. He said he was my deepest admirer.

"I will be here to see you off, cyclone."

Dear LJ,

I have no commitments to this man, only his promise of friendship with me. I am not quite sixteen, and that is enough for me. I could not have made it through this dark time without him. He witnessed what I had to endure that night. The horror of it will stay with me forever, but the love I felt that night will always remain special to me.

We manage to get through troubled times with the hope of a better tomorrow.

CHAPTER 25

Just Tell Her You Love Her

Flagstaff, Arizona Territory~June,1892
Age~15

I was sitting beside my bed at the rooming house when the door burst open. It was Tillie, and she was as upset as the day mama died. Tears were rolling down her face, and I could not understand anything she was saying.

"Calm down and tell me what is wrong." I handed her my hankie and immediately opened the drawer for another one. It did not look as if the flood would be over soon.

Finally, a word or two could be heard between sobs.

"Jesse," and then she sobbed, "he, he said he wants me to leave. He is trying to get rid of me. He doesn't love me anymore. He says I am still a child."

I did the one thing I had seen mama do with us when we were upset. I pulled her close to me to calm her down. After a few minutes, my shoulder was wet with tears. It was not as bad as I had imagined it would be consoling my sister. We have never been touchy people. Nellie has been telling us that we need more hugs. This isn't bad. I might get to like this hugging stuff.

I laid down beside her on the bed. She cried herself to sleep. I laid there until I was sure I could sneak out.

I closed the door to our room and went down the hall to Nellie's room. "Knock, Knock," I said, not wanting to wake the kids if they were napping.

My little niece, Nell, opened the door. She immediately hugged me.

Mama says that I am a big girl now. I am her big helper."

"Well, isn't that wonderful? I am proud of you."

I saw Nellie sitting in a chair with her head down. She looked up, and I could see she had been crying. Red blotches covered her face. Nellie has always gotten blotchy when she cries. I guess that would be her distinguishing characteristic.

I went to her and held her as I had just done with Tillie. I would be crying before I knew it if this kept going.

"Will someone please tell me what is going on today? Remember, yesterday we congratulated each other because none of us cried? We are three weeks since her death."

"I got a telegraph from Uncle Bernard today."

"Did he say no? Are we unwelcome at his home?"

"Calm down, Lizzie. He said yes and wants you to come immediately."

My heart raced, and I wanted to jump for joy. The new me composed myself, and I said, "Then why on earth is everyone crying? Shouldn't we be relieved?"

"Yes, we are. It is just happening sooner than we expected. Tillie is upset. She does not want to leave Jesse. She is afraid because he has not asked her to marry him yet. She thinks that if she leaves, he will find someone else."

"Is she daft?"

"Distraught. She is suffering deeper than we are right now. I just wish I could get Jesse to propose to her. That would make her feel more secure right now."

"Why were you crying when I came in? I mean, was it for mama?"

"No, I was feeling very sorry for myself for being put in this predicament. I do not like having to decide everything. The men are not helpful. George will come around, but right now, he is just trying to come to terms with her death. He is getting better. Bertie is drinking and fightin. So is Johnny. I cannot control them. Right now, I am so angry with them. I need them to pull themselves together and help me. It has been the hardest thing to do to send you two away right now."

"You can relax with me. I am anxious to go."

"Has Ed contacted you lately? Are you serious about him?"

I thought for a moment and said, "He gives me butterflies in my stomach. What does that mean?"

"Butterflies, eh? That is exactly how I felt with William." Nellie's face eased, and I swear her eyes twinkled as she told me about her feelings. "You cannot control it. You have no way of stopping it. Mama used to tell me that she had those same butterflies with daddy."

"You and mama were more like friends. You will miss her dearly. I cannot replace her, but I will always be here for you. I will try not be a thorn in your side."

We hugged. I learned that we do not need words to express how each other feels.

A knock came on the door, and it was Tillie. She didn't want to be alone right now.

I watched my sister, and a plan came into my head.

We ate our supper. The boarding house felt stuffy inside. I walked outside to cool off.

Jesse walked up and asked if Tillie was inside.

"Yeah, can I talk to you first?"

"Sure." Jesse did not talk much.

"If I may be abrupt for a minute, do you love my sister?"

"Yep."

"Have you told her?"

"She should know."

"How should she know?"

"Cause I'm still here."

"Do you have plans to marry her?'

"Yep."

"Have you asked her yet?"

"Nope."

"She would sure feel better if you asked her before we left for Michigan. I mean, she loves you."

"Okay."

"Nice talk, Jesse. Don't mention this talk to her, okay?"

"Sure enough." He tipped his hat and went inside. I shook my head, wondering if he had heard anything I said. Tillie can yack and yack to him all she wants, and is all he will do is give her one-word answers. Not a big conversationalist. I do not make a habit of interfering with relationships. I have not had enough experience myself. At this point, time would tell if my talk helped.

We hurriedly bought a couple of garments and undergarments to replace the ones we lost in the fire. We had to purchase a trunk to carry our clothing.

George announced that he would be traveling with us. Nellie said that he decided that it would help him if he got away. Michigan would be the answer.

I saw Ed and told him I was going.

"Are you coming back?"

"Yes, I plan to."

"I will see you then, cyclone. How old are you now? I can never remember."

"I will be sixteen in September."

"Go, enjoy yourself. You are only young and independent once. As for me, I am always unattached. I am a stag. No woman will get her tusks in me. I will be there at the train in the morning to see you off."

I was taken aback by his comments. Why was he telling me this? Is he warning me? It was all rather odd coming from a man like him.

Ed was at the train station as he had promised. Jesse was there, too. Odd, both men had flowers for each of us. Ed surprised me by pulling me close to him. My butterflies started a commotion in my stomach again. He whispered in my ear, "Pay no attention to my ranting; you know you mean the world to me, cyclone." He then kissed me on the lips.

I could feel Nellie's uneasiness. He did not ask for her or George's permission to be so bold.

We boarded the train. I, of course, had to have the window seat. We pulled out of the station, and I rushed to the back of the caboose to say good-bye to my mountain. I watched until she was out of sight. I will engrave her beauty into my brain.

Dear LJ,

We are off on our adventure. Just a few weeks ago, I never dreamed of leaving my town. Miss. Weatherford said I would be a world traveler. Here I go.

If hugs are life's blankets, we just need to wrap ourselves in them more often.

Train Ride East

Flagstaff, Arizona Territory
To Michigan~Summer To Fall 1892
Age~15–16

The train to Chicago was well on its journey. I noticed as I walked back inside from the caboose that the train was modern. It even smelled brand new.

I returned to my window seat. The flowers lay on my seat. I thought to myself, "What am I supposed to do with these on a train? I have no vase to place them in. Jewelry would have been nicer. Give me a gold necklace with filigree, something I can cherish."

Tillie was practically giddy over her flowers. Apparently, Jesse included a message on a card to her.

"What does it say?" You can tell me." I snidely looked around and said, "Who am I going to tell?"

"George."

I forgot about my older brother. He was already settled in with his hat covering his face, probably well on his way to slumber.

The conductor came by asking for our tickets. He punched a hole in the paper and proceeded to ask us where we were headed.

"Chicago and then on to Monroe, Michigan."

"You will be traveling for a few days. Have you ladies seen the club car? It gives you a wonderful view of the scenery. The dining car has delicious food. In Topeka, Kansas, we have a stopover, and you are encouraged to get out and enjoy the food from Mr. Fred Harvey. Just let me know personally if you need anything from me, and I will gladly see what I can do for you. This evening I will be readying the sleeping car for you. Welcome Aboard."

"Thank you; that all sounds lovely."

"Come on, Sis, let's go to the club car."

We made our way down the aisle toward the front of the train. Our bodies jerked back and forth with the motion of the train. When we passed through the doors to the other car, we could smell food. Yum. I would be the first in line for lunch.

We went to the club car. The windows were large, and there was ample seating.

"This is where you can find me when I am not in the dining car," I said, scurrying to a chair. "These are so comfortable. Look, they turn around. We can face each other to talk to one another."

Tillie scowled at me, meaning she was in no mood for talking right now.

There were more people our age up here than in the cars below. People like George were content to stay in their seats.

I rode up there until the conductor came through with an announcement for lunch.

George and Tillie were entering the dining car from the other end, just as I was coming down. Tillie and I loved the dining car with its starched white tablecloths and a rose on each table.

We took our seat. The menu listed several food items. Pate duckling with crackers, toast cups a 'la chicken, and bread pudding for dessert, among other things. We ordered from the waiter and ate our meal.

George sat with us. He seemed different. Refined. He ordered the pork medallions with red potatoes. I watched his mannerisms change from the time we got on the train. He was almost giddy. Apparently, this way of life suits him. He left the dusty, dirty cowboy behind and was a very handsome man dressed up.

When I returned to the club car, there was a group of young people playing cards. Immediately, they asked me if I played bridge.

"Only a few times, but I am a fast learner."

We played several hands until I realized that we were in New Mexico. I must see my old home and look for Fort Wingate.

When we stopped at the Fort, I could see people getting on. I wonder if they know the Hathaway's. They are no longer there, but they might have known of them. I would ask if given the opportunity.

Later, I went down to our car and saw George talking with a lady. She looked familiar. George was talking and laughing. I could not believe my eyes. I said something to Tillie, and she expressed the same thoughts as me. Is this our George?

It came to me that she was the postmaster's wife from McCarty's. I do remember George spending a lot of time at the post office.

"What if George had a life we didn't know about?" I whispered to Tillie.

"Good for him. He deserves a life. Raising all of us has made him crotchety. He needed this trip as much as we do." We had never thought a lot about the sacrifice he had made for us. We took George for granted.

I sat down to write in LJ. As I wrote, I wondered about the card that Jesse gave Tillie with her flowers.

When she got up to stretch and use the ladies' powder room, I quickly glanced through her things. She must have the note on her. Not that I am a nosey person, just curious. A quick glance would satisfy my curiosity. Maybe later.

Most of the day was spent listening for the conductor to name the town we were coming upon. I was most curious. I began to make a note in LJ as to the names of towns. People came and went. I had never been on a train this long before. I could get claustrophobic if I thought about it; I did not allow myself the opportunity.

George sat beside the woman he spent the afternoon talking with. He seemed to like her company.

Tillie and I agreed to keep his socialization to ourselves.

We were surprised to find our seats made into beds when we returned from dinner.

I got the top bed, and she was below me on the bottom. The heavy drapery provided privacy. I watched out the window, staring into the dark terrain. The train stopped on the tracks for a long time. Boredom must have overcome me, and I could sleep.

We were in Kansas when I awoke. I thought back to my past when I walked this vast prairie beside the wagon train. My how life has changed. This is the way I like to travel.

We exited the train in Topeka. The conductor told us that he would be leaving us here, but another would be coming on duty.

"Do you live here?" I asked.

"No, my home is in Los Angeles. I will sleep over and tomorrow ride the train west."

We were very impressed with the restaurant. Young women dressed in like uniforms, black skirts, and aprons neatly starched with a white blouse underneath served our lunch. No detail to perfection was overlooked. We were told that they only employed single women. They are very strict with the girls. They live in dormitories provided by the company. If you break the rules, you are automatically dismissed from service. No exceptions, worse than being a nun, I thought to myself. If things went downhill, I could always join these ladies.

The rest of the trip seemed rather monotonous. I was getting eager to arrive in Chicago. From there, we would change trains and head to Grand Rapids. The family would pick us up there. I understand that we will be meeting other families from the surrounding area.

George's lady friend was going through to Chicago. We did not see much of him.

The arrival at the train station was overwhelming, to say the least. It was so big, and I had never seen so many people in my whole life. We felt small and insignificant.

George was now attentive and in a fine disposition. He took charge of us, stowing our baggage in a compartment that we rented for a few cents.

We walked outside and down the street. We were surprised to see a river flowing between the streets. It is called the Chicago River. It was hot, and I was feeling very sticky and uncomfortable.

George explained that this was humidity. Where our air out west is dry; theirs is wet.

Beads of sweat gathered on my forehead. I noticed that my hair was curling more than usual.

It did not take us long to be immersed in the city. There were ladies wearing banners across their fronts, campaigning for Women's rights. The city was preparing for the World's Fair the following year. We could see the buildings going up for the big event. A very tall wheel-like object could be seen from a distance. Someone called it a Ferris wheel.

We bought fresh taffy made on machine and popcorn covered in caramel with peanuts.

Sadly, we had to make our way back to the depot. I would have loved to have stayed and seen more, but we had a train to catch.

This train was not as impressive as the one we had ridden earlier.

We reached Grand Rapids by mid-afternoon the next day. Tillie and I were both a little nervous. George, however, seemed calm.

We were surprised to see a large crowd gathered to meet us. We had no idea we had that much family. As someone told us, this isn't nearly all of them.

Our adventure begins.

Dear LJ,

What a trip. I love traveling. The family we met seemed happy to see us. George knows all the older ones. Again, Tillie and I were amazed at how happy he seemed. He was back home. Everyone wanted to know all about us and what life was like where we were from.

I shall keep you informed.

Don't judge people by where they are from; we are all from somewhere else.

CHAPTER 27

A Whirlwind Summer

Monroe, Michigan~1892
Age~15+

After the train pulled away from the station in Grand Rapids, Michigan, I felt my stomach turn. It is one thing to talk about traveling but entering the unknown made me nervous. However, George had a spring in his step that we were not used to seeing. He seemed almost giddy as he stepped off the train.

The station was crowded with people. More than I was used to.

Introductions were made as soon as we disembarked. There was so much commotion going on around us. My head was spinning with names. How would I possibly remember who was who and from which side of the family? Since Hoffman's had married Sturn's, several people could claim lineage on both sides. It felt odd to share a family with strangers.

We stayed around Grand Rapids for several days. Meeting the elderly relatives who had a difficult time traveling.

Tillie and I told George that we had to see the church where mama and daddy were married.

"We've gone past it every day we have been here. Why didn't you say something earlier?"

"Tomorrow is Sunday. We will go to church service."

"I have never been to a non-Catholic church," I said.

"There are similarities between the two. There are priests in both, but Episcopalian Priests can be married."

"I want to go," Tillie said in an almost demanding voice. "Jesse is Episcopalian."

My ears perked up. I wanted to pressure her, but it is not appropriate right now.

St. Mark's Episcopalian Church was the most beautiful church I had ever seen during my life. Tillie was awe-struck.

As we entered, I had goose pimples up and down my arm. I felt as though both mama and daddy were beside me.

The family had no idea that we even knew about the church.

"Mama told us many things about her life in Michigan. Daddy did not speak much about it in fear of making mama homesick."

George spoke up and said, "Daddy felt guilty for taking her away from her family."

An older relative said that "Adam should have felt guilty. Dragging a woman who was with child off to the middle of nowhere wasn't right."

He was quickly quieted by others standing around. Tillie kicked my foot underneath the table, warning me to mind my p's and q's. She knew that I might speak my mind and defend our father.

We wasted no time after arriving in Monroe to become the most popular attraction. The social lives of city people were so busy; every day was filled with engagements. I swear; I never figured out when they worked. Uncle Bernard did; we only saw him in the evenings at dinner.

Everyone's curiosity for us must have been the draw to attend these ridiculous things. After a couple of these extravagant dinner parties, I had my fill. I am not able to refuse to attend. As Tillie told me, I would be insulting the family's generosity.

It was almost a relief to be sent to bed because it was my time of the month. I wonder why I would have one now. It is so seldom that I even have one.

I often thought of mama and tried to picture her here. Life was so different, and she never complained. I only know of a couple of times she took herself to bed because of her cycle. A woman on the prairie or ranch did not have that luxury.

George went out today and returned with two new suits. He has not indicated to either of us how long he will stay.

George is also spending his afternoons at the Men's Club. Since it is for men only, no woman knows what goes on in there. What if the women had a club where no men were allowed?

Since receiving the letter from Lettie telling me about the Women's Vote movement and the Temperance Movement, my curiosity has sparked. I had to hold myself back from running over to them, grabbing a sign, and marching alongside these brave women. Courageous. They are covered in tomatoes or garbage that is thrown at them while they march. Lettie told me about women being arrested. I know that I will be following them while I am here. Who knows, possibly I will get a chance to participate. On second thought, perhaps I should wait until we leave, and I visit Lettie in Chicago. I could not bear to disappoint Uncle Bernard. If my name appeared in the local newspaper for marching, I would disgrace the family, and I would not want to do that.

There was so much going on in the world that I didn't even know about. My curiosity was aroused.

We were taken out to a dress shop. Here we were measured and fitted for new dresses. Tillie kept saying that we could not pay for the garments. Auntie told us that it was no concern of ours. Uncle Bernard could spend money on his nieces. Then out came the hats, gloves, necklaces, undergarments, stockings, and shoes. We were dumbfounded. Clothes had always come from mama. We were offered tea and cakes while we were shopping. Can you imagine?

We rode bicycles all around a gorgeous green grass park. I had never seen grass before like this. I ran around in it whenever I could get away with my bare feet. We had picnics in the middle of the week.

I met a young man. His name was Stephen. He kept coming to the park where we frequented. It started with a simple hello. He would laugh when I rode by on my bicycle. Of course, I rode by him often. I was teasing him, egging him on. Okay, I was learning to flirt. Maybe some girls automatically know how to do that, but I had to practice.

The first time we spoke, I waited for the butterflies to come. There were none. Odd, I liked him; he smiled and laughed. The butterflies shy and were hiding.

Auntie knew the young man well. His family was prominent in the town. She permitted us to walk together if we could be seen by her.

He was very curious about my upbringing in the wild west. I told him how I won a shooting match given by Buffalo Bill Cody.

"Have you fought savages?"

I laughed and told him that there were no savages. They are all people, and most were very kind. What would he think of me if he knew the things that I have done? I should think he would call me a savage.

He was a guest at the next dinner party. George decided to announce that evening that he would be returning home.

He had an opportunity to purchase some land north of town around Mr. Schultz. He told Tillie and me later it involved Mr. Shroyer. Bill had returned to town after being gone on a gold-mining expedition for several months. The man was in shock at the news of mama. George was going back to console him. He had difficulty finding anyone who knew where we were. Dr. Brannen gave him our address, so a telegram could be sent.

Uncle Bernard said it was too bad that we would not have a telephone anytime soon out west. Their telephone was to be installed next week.

George packed up and returned home. We will miss him. Tillie whispered something into his ear, and he assured her that he would take care of it for her.

What is she up to? She mentioned nothing to me. After George left, Tillie became quite close to one of our cousins. The girl was getting married next year. Tillie was excited to help with the planning of the ceremony. I had never heard of a wedding taking a year to plan. Didn't you just decide to do it and get it over with?

I found other things to keep me occupied. Stephen's family had a series of canals that were used to transport goods. He took me on a canal boat when he went to inspect it for obstructions. The beaver was often the culprit of such blockages. He would next mark the location and put it in his log. What surprised me was that he did not take care of the problem right then. When he returned to the office, one of the employees was sent out to clear the canal. I wanted to tell him how I would run his business and not waste precious time. I would have preferred to watch him clean the canal while he was there, instead of wasting time having someone else do the job he could have done.

Others used the canals to transport goods, and they would pay his family for the right of access. My mind questioned; how can you charge someone for using water?

If this was an example of this man's workday, he would never survive in the West. I was becoming less interested in him as the days went on.

I began to point out things to him that he could do differently with his business. He, of course, argued that he was just a small part of the decision making. There would come a day when he would manage the business, but as far as he was concerned, that was a long time away. He sounded rather curt when he told me that I had no inkling as to what his business was about or how to run it.

Obviously, he had no inkling who I was and what I did know. Nor did he have any desire to find out.

I immediately made a mental notation that he had insulted me.

On one of our walks in the park, I noticed a group of women gathering for a women's march. I asked Stephen if we could walk over towards the ladies. I was hoping to make their acquaintance and tell them I supported the movement.

Stephen became very irate with me. He demanded that I turn around.

"Lizzie, do as I say. I forbid you to expose yourself to the likes of those floozies."

"Excuse me? You have no authority over me." I continued walking towards the women.

"I implore you to obey me this instant, or I shall be forced to tell your uncle."

"Tell my uncle what? That I wished to ask a group of women to educate me on the suffragette movement?"

"Why, yes. Then I shall tell him how you disobeyed my request when I told you to stop."

"If you perceived me as a female who can be led about the park on a leash and bark orders at me as if I would be a dog, you are sadly mistaken. Good-day, Stephen."

I turned and walked away. I excused myself from my aunt's company and asked to return to their home.

Of all the impertinent ideas that man has. Who does he think he is? My blood was boiling.

Lucky for me, we were not having a dinner party tonight.

I begged off from going to the park the next day. My absence would surely be noticed.

My aunt returned home with an envelope for me from Stephen. She knew that we had a tiff.

I took the envelope and went to my room to read my mail.

My dearest Lizzie,

It appears to me that I have injured your feelings. It was not my intent to do so. I was merely trying to protect your naivety of acceptable behavior in public. An honorable woman would accept their place in society and be quite content, letting the men take the lead.

We can discuss your actions further at our next meeting.

Your friend and admirer,

Stephen Gurley

I crumpled the letter in my fists and threw it into the flames of the fire burning in the stove.

"That is what I think of you, sir." I said out loud, "If it is up to me, there shall be no next time…."

Dear LJ,

This man claiming to be my friend has insulted my integrity. He thinks that I shall do his beck and call. Am I not allowed to make my own decisions as to who I will and will not talk to?

He is not my father, and cannot order me around. Besides, it is not love that I feel for this man. He was but a friend who was hiding his true self behind a mask. He revealed to me who he was, and I can no longer be his friend.

People are an interesting breed. I feel I have learned more about how complicated life can be.

Be wary of someone who calls you their friend but does not respect you for who you are.

CHAPTER 28

A Lavish Sixteenth Birthday

Monroe, Michigan~4th September,1892
Age~16

As my big day approached for the much-anticipated sixteenth birthday, I became very homesick. Tillie was busy helping our cousin with her wedding plans. I personally did not understand why she was spending so much time helping her when we would not be here to see it through. At least, I would not be nearby. Home is all I think about.

As for Tillie, I could not see her staying away from Jesse any longer than necessary. I did know that she pined for him. The two girls could be overheard discussing their men. I was still fuming over the way Stephen had treated me.

He did not stop pursuing me. I was the one who had stopped answering his letters.

I was well hidden at the top of the immense staircase listening while he was at the front door. He sounded pathetic as he complained to my aunt about my shunning him. I suppose he expected her to order me to accompany him to the park. There, he explained, he could convince me to forgive him for speaking out of line.

"She is a strong young lady with a very inquisitive mind of her own. She reminds me of her dear father. Once she sets her mind on something, there is no changing it. What I have seen of her is conclusive of how her mother used to describe her to me in her letters. I have no reason to question her tenacity. I will leave it to her to decide the course of your friendship. Good day, Mr. Gurley. She promptly closed the door.

I stood silent for a moment and reveled in my aunt's words. I decided to return to my room. I knew I had to tell LJ about this phenomenal event.

Tomorrow it would be my sixteenth birthday. I reminisce on past birthdays. I did not anticipate any sort of to do. I did not mention my birthday to anyone here in the house and decided that Tillie was far too involved in other matters to remember my birthday.

I went down to dinner, finding that everyone was predisposed for the evening except my aunt.

It was our first time to be alone together. We visited with each other in general conversation. She asked me how I was coping with being away from home.

I answered her honestly, not seeing any reason to skirt around the subject. I am homesick, I confessed to her. I missed many things from home.

"What is it that you miss the most, my dear? Maybe there is something we can do to remind you of home."

I laughed and said, "If you can create my mountain for me, then I shall be happy."

"A mountain? We have hills but few mountains. I understand that yours is tall and very majestic looking."

"Yes, how did you know?"

"Your mother, dear. She spoke of it often in her letters. She said that just to gaze upon it brought her peace in her life."

"I never knew that we shared our love for the mountain." My eyes got teary thinking of what we both enjoyed. I told my aunt about climbing the water tower and sitting on top of the world with my friend gazing at the mountain in the moonlight.

We sat and visited, laughed, and cried together for the rest of the evening. I was not feeling so alone when I tucked myself in bed for the last time of being fifteen. Tomorrow would be a new start to a new year. There was no part of me that would miss being fifteen again.

I said my prayers and wrote a few lines in LJ, telling her about my visit with my aunt. I also wished LJ a happy birthday. I have had her for six years now.

The sun shone brightly on this September morning. I awoke to a knock on my door. It was Tillie bringing me breakfast in bed.

"What is this? I feel like royalty, eating in bed."

"It is your birthday, and you are sixteen. Nellie told me to do something special for our little sister today. What is it that you would like to do today?"

"I would love to go to the River Raisin Battlefield. It was a battlefield in the war of 1812. It was an awful attack on us. We lost the battle. Daddy said after the big war, he found peace in going to the River Raisin and sitting on the banks, reflecting his time in the war. I have wanted to go down there and see it. That is all I want for my birthday."

"You are easily pleased, my sister. I will go downstairs and see if that can be arranged. Now get dressed."

I went downstairs to find the house quiet. Tillie was in the kitchen waiting for me. A nice wicker basket was waiting on the table filled with various items for our lunch. My mind went back to Rosita and her wonderful tortillas and beans. Oh, how I missed those.

The carriage driver was waiting for us as we walked outside. I forgot my hat upstairs, and as I went inside to get it, I thought I saw someone step from sight. Odd, I thought.

I called out, "Who is here?" No answer. It must have been my imagination.

I climbed into the leather tufted seat in the carriage. We left the house to begin our adventure. I could smell the leather.

"Do you smell it, Tillie? The aromatic smell of leather."

"I don't smell anything," she replied, sniffing the air.

"Funny, I don't smell it now either. It was always daddy's smell. Maybe he is a ghost and riding with us today."

"Don't be silly. You know I don't believe in ghosts and omens and premonitions."

"You wouldn't be afraid of daddy, would you?"

"No, of course not."

"I guess I just feel nostalgic today."

We traveled along the banks of Lake Erie. We commented on how large it was and that we had never seen a lake that substantial before in our lives. We also laughed at how close we were to the state of Ohio. We could look across and see another state. How odd was that? Miss Weatherford would be saying, "I told you that you would see the world."

We walked along the banks of the River Raisin. We sat down on benches that were strategically placed. We ate our lunch on a blanket that had been thoughtfully placed in the carriage for us. It was a different way of life.

"Tillie, do you wish you could stay here forever?"

"No, it is fine for a short time, but I miss being home."

"Do you? Me too; I thought you wanted to stay."

"No, not even if Jesse moved here. We are from the west. The sky is bluer out west than over in this place, and there are no mountains. Flagstaff is our home. I miss our family. I even miss Johnny."

We laughed and visited like the old days. I was happy. Down at the bottom of the lunch basket were two special pieces of chocolate candy from our favorite candy shop. Just the littlest of things can make you happy.

We returned home later in the afternoon. The evening bustle to get dinner on the table for Uncle Bernard was in full swing. As they rushed me past the drawing-room, I again thought I saw someone hiding from vision.

I went upstairs to my room; there, a nice hot bath was waiting. The maid told me I smelled like the river and that Uncle Bernard would not appreciate that at his table. I soaked in the warm bath that smelled of roses. The washbasin was a large brass tub. It was so highly polished that you could see your face in the shine.

When I got out, I was told my aunt had a new dress made, especially for the occasion.

"What occasion? I asked.

"Your birthday, ma'am."

"Are we having a special dinner tonight for me?"

"I can't be letting go of any secrets. Is all I know and don't you go telling anyone I informed you, is that the Mrs. has gone all out for you tonight." She said, pointing her finger at me as she talked.

"Thank you. I shall not tell a soul."

Never has it taken me so much time to get dressed.

The maid placed rouge upon my cheek, and then she placed it on my lips. It was a radiant rosy red. She stopped to look and complimented me on how good-looking I was tonight. My hair was styled up on my head, and ribbon with beads was placed around the curls. I wore a pink ribbon around my neck with a gold filigree brooch pinned in the middle of my neck. I was even given new pink shoes to match the dress. Of course, shoes are always put on before the dress; otherwise, you would not be able to bend over to put them on your feet. Next came the corsets and petticoats. The very last thing was to dress in the beautiful pink and white dress.

As I gazed into the floor-length mirror, I did not recognize the woman who looked back at me. I was beautiful.

I left the room with Tillie, who was dressed as gorgeous as I had ever seen her.

We walked down the stairs to a darkened entranceway.

"Surprise" was shouted, and candles lit to reveal a houseful of people who had come to help me celebrate turning sixteen. That would explain why people were hiding from me earlier in the day.

I was dumbstruck. I thanked everyone for coming. We proceeded to go into the dining room. A lavish meal was set out. I had my first taste of champagne as I was toasted and sang to.

Then we proceeded to the ballroom. Guests came up to me with hugs and flowers. Other guests arrived after dinner. There were far too many for them all to be invited to dinner.

I saw Stephen sitting with his parents. They had just arrived. He avoided looking at me, or so I thought. When he thought I didn't see him, and I spotted him staring at me.

I was standing alone trying to adjust the uncomfortable girdle that women are forced to wear when someone said to me, "Hey cowgirl, want to teach me how to rope a calf?"

I nearly jumped out of my skin. It was my dear cousin Jacob, who came to stay with us in New Mexico. I hugged him and was excited to see him again. He introduced Tillie and me to his wife and three children.

I whispered to him that I now knew how he felt in our neck of the woods, out of place.

Stephen finally got up the nerve to come over to me and try to apologize. I was polite but offered no apology in return.

He asked if he could see me tomorrow, and I told him no. We were no more compatible than a mouse and a rattlesnake living in the same hole. I am the rattlesnake, and I would eat the mouse.

I did get to visit with Jacob over the next few days. We reminisced and laughed. I did get a few baby butterflies in my stomach when I first saw him, but they quickly dissipated when I met his charming wife.

Tillie and I began talking among ourselves about returning home. Sometimes, you just know when it is time to leave. We did not want to overstay our welcome.

We left on the train from Grand Rapids to Chicago.

There, waiting for us, was Lettie and her mother. We stayed in their apartment in Chicago.

We were both amazed at how each of us had grown up.

She introduced us to her radical female friends who just wanted a say in how the country was run. It seemed like such an easy thing to do. Why were men making it so hard?

I was sad to leave my friend but anxious to be home.

Dear LJ,

A much-needed trip helped ease the pain of my loss. I met new people and saw new things. I can now see in my mind the beautiful church where my parents were married. I can picture a lake as big as an ocean. However, nothing can even come close to my mountain.

Learning that others love what you enjoy is only found out by communication.

Mr. Al Gregg, father and father-in-law of Jesse and Tillie Gregg
The picture is Property of JK Hoffman

CHAPTER 29

Mrs. Jesse Gregg

Flagstaff, Arizona Territory~
October-November~1892
Age~16

The train pulled into Flagstaff on an overcast Monday afternoon. As we stepped off, the wind blew around me, practically taking me over. I glanced around and watched the leaves blow down the tracks. It was almost as if something was trying to tell me something. A warning, maybe? I felt as if it was saying to me, "Get back on the train keep going, don't get off."

Before I could have time to think, Georgie and little Nell came running up to Tillie and me. Our first urge was to pick them up and twirl them around. However, they had grown up so much it took us by surprise.

The family then came out from inside the station to greet us. We rushed inside out of the cold. Jesse was there waiting for Tillie. He was all dressed up, at least for a westerner. Then I looked at his suit and realized that this was one of the suits that George had bought back in Monroe. It all came together like a puzzle in my head. Tillie had George go to the tailor and had a suit made for Jesse.

The family huddled around us so tight that you could not see who was there. We had to hug everyone. When the greetings were over, I frantically looked around for Ed. He would normally be holding back, letting the family have their time with us, and he would make his way up to me. He must be here. Maybe he stepped out at the wrong time.

Bert, as he preferred to be called now, was anxiously waiting to show us his new nine-passenger carriage. He is working as a drayman; he carries passengers and goods to wherever anyone needs them to go. We were all very impressed by his carriage.

Everyone was getting themselves seated but me. I did not want to ask anyone about Ed because I just knew in my heart that he would be here waiting for me. Even our luggage was put on before I got inside.

Jokes were made about how many trunks we left with and how many more we brought back with us.

Tillie and Jesse got in the very back row of seats. Tillie was holding on to him as if she did not dare to let him go. They made such a cute couple.

I sat next to Nellie, Nell, and Georgie. We were a little cramped, but no one complained. My eyes could not help but search the streets for Ed as we made our way up to Gold Avenue. We turned onto Fine Street, our old neighborhood. There, waiting for us, was our brand-new house.

The local men in town erected a new house for us, just down the street from the old one. The women in town decorated the house with a female touch. Mrs. Miller was waiting anxiously with Boots and the cow for me.

Again, I thought maybe Ed would be there to surprise me with a bouquet of flowers or something. He was nowhere to be seen.

Nellie must have known something because she kept looking at me. What did she know that I did not?

The townsfolk had prepared a big meal for us, and the party seemed to last way too long into the night.

The next day, Nellie came to me and asked me what was wrong. I replied, 'Nothing."

"Are you upset that Ed Geddes did not make an appearance?"

"Why? Should he have been here? He probably had not been told I was coming in yesterday. Normally, the men would have gotten in touch with him. He is like a part of my family."

"I know, but he is not the man for you."

"How would you know when I don't even know myself?"

"I have grown up around men like him all my life. He is a loner, and he will break your heart."

"It is my heart that will be broken and not yours."

"I think that you should know that after you left, I saw him and told him not to come around. You are too vulnerable right now, and he agreed."

"Thank you for telling me. Now, I know who to blame."

"I am just looking out for you. You are my responsibility now. We will get through this together."

I could not blame her. She did not ask to become my mother; she was thrown into the position by tragedy.

Tillie and Jesse spared no time in announcing their marriage. Jesse had purchased land and had begun building a home for the two of them. It was three miles north of town with a gorgeous view of the mountain. Although the family acted surprised, most had suspected that a union would take place in the future, just not as soon as November.

Honestly, though, I will be relieved when they are married. Poor Tillie is beside herself with worry feeling it is improper to marry so quickly. She should not care what others think. I do not care.

As usual, the dilemma came as to what to do about me. I see no problem at all in my living in the new house. I can cook and take care of my brothers just fine. They know my dislike for the domestic side and balk at the idea of me being responsible for the home. They announced there were many good eateries in town that they could get food at and that it would taste like food, they teased. Usually, I would have pouted and runoff, off; however, now a refined woman, and I would not act in my old way.

As for now, the family has agreed not to decide until after Tillie and Jesse's wedding day. Bert, Tillie, I will live in the new house. George will remain in Bellemont on his farm.

Nellie and Tillie tell me that they suspect there is something wrong with me. Ha, ha, I know what you are thinking. I am not crazy. I mean, with my female parts. They are concerned because my "flow" is so irregular. Apparently, I should be plagued with that bothersome nuisance once a month. I barely have had one since mama died. Nellie says she worries that one day when I marry and want to have children, I may not be able to have any. They are both quite concerned for me, but I am not. Maybe it is my youth, and I am naïve as they claim. Time will tell.

Wedding plans were coming along for Tillie. She spends most of her time out at the cabin site. Now that the snow has fallen, it is good that it is nearly complete. I rode out with her in the buggy the other day to watch its progression. I share in her excitement. She will make Jesse the perfect wife.

Our Auntie in Michigan had a beautiful gown made for her. It did not, in any way, violate the rules of mourning. The family sent their blessing and wished they could have seen her get married. She made a stunning bride. She had a few moments of tears for mama and daddy before she walked down the aisle.

In respect of the family still being in mourning for Mama, it was a small affair performed in the Episcopalian Church on Leroux Street with a few friends and family attending. Tillie has converted to Episcopalian, of course, denying the fact that it had anything to do with the exquisite Episcopal church in Michigan that we had visited.

Tillie and Jesse live in their new home north of town. The cabin is small now, but it will do nicely. Tillie has insisted on a honeymoon for a few nights at the Grand Canyon.

Exciting news, Nellie is expecting another baby. Mama would have been so delighted. The railroad has transferred William back to

Yucca. Poor Nellie can never make a permanent home anywhere. At least, she is closer to us.

As for me, I think I will enjoy living almost alone. Bert is here, but you know how men are; he is never there.

I have my animals to keep me company, along with friends. Ed has not come around. I guess Nellie put the fear of God into him. Coward.

LJ,

Why are all the men I meet chicken livers? Are they afraid of me? I just can't figure them out. There are good ones, and then there are not so good ones. I think Tillie got a good one. Weddings bring tears, for some reason, I can't understand. As for Tillie, I understand, with the wedding being so close to mama's tragic accident.

To witness true love is like watching God's greatest gift unfold. Beautiful.

Young Hoffman children Ella Hoffman
and Floyd Hoffman on a tree stump. Circa 1905
The picture is Property of JK Hoffman

CHAPTER 30

Lizzie Meets an Old Friend

Flagstaff, Arizona Territory~1893
Age~17

I am on my own now. Life is certainly different compared to my old life when mama was here, and we were a family. I am an orphan. I never dreamed that a family as big as ours could go in so many directions. Losing both of my parents in tragic ways leaves a hole in my heart. I have no choice but to protect and look out for myself. 'My independence,' that is what I like to call it. At least, I have my siblings when I need someone.

Tillie is busy settling into married life with Jesse. I envy her at times that she is happy with being a woman. She accepts her daily chores as normal. I feel that I will never be content raising a family and looking after someone. After all, I am the youngest in the family, so I am used to going about on my own. Tillie, on the other hand, is very organized in her life. She was, after all, Mama's right hand. I laughed because when mama used to say that, I would giggle and say something inappropriate. Looking back, I now see that I was jealous of their relationship.

I had that with Daddy but not mama. I wish Daddy were still alive. I could learn a lot from him. He always seemed so sure of himself. He was never afraid to take on new endeavors. After all, he went from being a shoe cobbler in Michigan to a farmer in Kansas and on to ranching in New Mexico. He enjoyed being an American. Owning his land was the most important thing to him. I feel the same way. If only I could become a rancher.

My brothers say that it is hard to own a ranch. They seem to prefer life with no attachments or commitments. They have few people that they answer to daily. Riding the ranges on horseback, sometimes alone, is satisfying for them. They have their entertainment in town, with everyone expecting them to act disruptive and obnoxious. Johnny, especially, likes to be wild. George likes solace. Bertie likes to fight just for the sake of fighting. He should be a boxer in a ring with a crowd of people cheering him on with every blow to his opponent. He could be famous like John L. Sullivan for fighting.

I have my own job; I am working as a shop clerk. I get my own money to spend or save as I like.

Tillie and I were invited to attend a gala event in town. It was a bridal shower for an old friend. We just knew we had to get her something wonderful. A gift bought in Chicago. We contacted Lettie and asked her to go to the best department store in the city. Shop as if it were her getting married, and what would she enjoy?

She picked out a pair of sterling silver candle holders. Perfect. She agreed to even have them gift-wrapped and mailed to us for the occasion.

If I do say so myself, our gift was the most elaborate candle holders she received. Unfortunately, she received several pairs. Really now, can one have too many candle holders?

Tillie can rarely go with me to anything. I miss her company.

Tonight, I am going with friends to Winslow for a dance. We boarded the train headed east, and soon we arrived at our destination. All the girls are adorned in their finest dresses, including me. I have always enjoyed the feel of dancing around a room filled with people.

Sometimes it is girls dancing with girls. Men are afraid to do that kind of thing.

I can smell gardenia on one of my friends. My favorite smell. I close my eyes and take in the sweet smell. My toilet water, Eau de toilette, as it is said in French, is not as sweet-smelling as hers. I shall have to buy gardenia or jasmine next time. I will make a mental note of that.

We arrived early, so I took a few moments alone to remember back to my first trip here from Albuquerque. I love to look out over the vastness and see the outlines of the mesas, far off in the distance. The wind is blowing at quite a pace. It is blowing my skirt up.

We decide to go into the little café in town. The girls were seated by the time I came into the chophouse. A young girl, with her head down, was busy working. She seemed out of sorts.

I did not pay her any mind but sat with my friends and socialized with each other. We were rather loud with our laughing and talking. We became more aware of our surroundings as the place began to fill with other guests.

Suddenly, without warning, chills ran down my spine. I felt as if I were being stared at, not just a random person watching me, but someone glaring at me. Nervously, I glanced around the room. Hoping there might be someone I know or recognize. No one, in fact, everyone seemed to be engaged with their own group of friends. I decide it is just me being silly. I can hear Tillie's voice in my head saying, "Oh Lizzie; you are such a foolish girl."

As we go to leave the cafe, a gust of wind blows fine particles of sand into our faces. My teeth feel as if I just ate a bowl of sand for dinner. My hair falls, encircling my face.

"Oh no, we cannot go to the dance looking like this." squealed several of the girls.

I went back to the cafe and over to the girl working there. "Excuse me, is there a place where we can freshen up?"

Our eyes met, and I recognized her immediately. "I know you!" I blurt out suddenly. Embarrassed with myself, I quickly cupped my hand over my mouth and mumbled to please excuse my rudeness. I could feel my cheeks turn red in embarrassment.

Without speaking a word, she took me up to some stairs in the corner of the cafe. They were very narrow stairs, as were often the case for the hired help. We entered a tiny dark room upstairs. Glancing around quickly, I noticed there was only a neatly made bed and a small dresser and chair. There are no decorations about the room except a little mirror and a water pitcher and bowl.

"Is this your room?"

"Yes. Now, you must excuse me as I must get back downstairs. Help yourself to the towel in the top dresser drawer."

"Wait, please, I don't even know your name."

"Belle, my name is Belle. And yours?"

Again, shivers ran up my spine.

"Lizzie."

"We have met before, Lizzie. Do you remember me?"

"Yes, yes, I do. I met you in Santa Fe at the Loretto School. You were nice to me. You gave me the black onyx horse. Do you remember?"

Suddenly, there was a loud knocking on the door and a voice calling for Belle.

"I have to go now," she said hurriedly. She excused herself and ran out of the door.

I finished washing up and remembered leaving the girls out on the street. As I made my way down the small stairs, I could hear loud voices shouting at each other from the kitchen. I wanted to find her and thank her for the use of her room. I heard sobs and a "No; I was just helping a customer wash up."

I left to find that the girls had gone on without me. Fair enough since I rather deserted them. I made my way to the dance. I felt as if I had just created trouble for the poor girl. I could not help but think about my chance encounter with her after so many years. It seemed as if a lifetime had passed since I had seen her. Moreover, I want to ask her about her premonition about the black horse and a man in my future.

Hoping to find her, I left the dance early and returned to the chophouse. Inquiring about her, they informed me that they had dismissed her. "No," I said, "It was my fault for detaining her. I need to find her. Where is she?"

A shrug of the shoulder and a hand gesture shooing me away was all I got out of the man.

With a heavy heart, I headed off toward the station. I got the poor girl dismissed from her job. My heart was sick.

I had to speak with the owner and explain to him that it was all my fault. I turned and ran back to the cafe.

"You must listen to me," I blurted out in front of the customers. "It was not her fault. I detained her, and she was too polite to leave. Please, sir, you must find her and give her job back to her. I insist." At that instant, I heard the train whistle announcing its arrival. I had no option but to leave without finding her.

The train ride home seemed longer than usual. We had our merriment at the dance, and I suppose I am just feeling let down after all the excitement of the evening. I close my eyes and try to sleep. I find myself thinking of Belle and feeling very guilty if I am to be the reason for her dismissal.

Sarah, a friend of mine, assured me that there must be more to it than Belle letting me freshen up inside her room. Perhaps she wanted to be dismissed? I hope she can find work elsewhere.

It was chance that brought us together briefly, and it would be a chance if I ever saw her again. I vowed to make it up to her if, in any circumstances, I saw her once more.

Summer is an exceptional season on the mountain. I enjoy riding my horse with friends. There is usually a group of us that ride north towards the mountain. Trees have been cut down by the timber companies, leaving snags, about three feet high or taller, sticking out of the ground. Some of these are rather large around. As we rode toward Jesse and Tillie's cabin, we encountered several of these near one another, making it difficult to maneuver the horses around.

Unfortunately, riding off the dirt road was made nearly impossible for fear of the horse falling over one of the snags.

We could hear a ruckus up ahead. The men were working very diligently on something in the ground. As we neared, we could see that the men were trying to remove the stump. It was apparent to us that they were clearing the land for a cabin. The men had shovels and picks that they were using to dig around the stump. It seemed like very laborious work, with little progress being made.

We waved as we made our way through the workers. One man, whom it was obvious that he was very rude, catcalled to us. We ignored him and rode on our way.

After we were a distance up the road, we all started to giggle about the man who was catcalling. Any girl likes the thought of a man thinking she is good-looking.

We followed the river bottom northwesterly towards 'The San Francisco Springs.' Here we could enjoy the shade and get a cool drink of water. The canyon walls, although not very high, made you feel as if you were secluded from the world.

We tied the horses up to a tree and opened our baskets to enjoy our lunch. Why does food taste better when you are out in nature?

We sat playing a game of whist and old maid. I won most of the games because I am competitive. In other words, I do not like to lose. We also played a game of chase and hide-and-go-seek. I hid so well in a thicket that the other girls started to panic. They declared me the winner if I came out of hiding. Of course, I took my own sweet time about it, not wanting to appear as if I could be easily persuaded.

We realized that none of us had a timepiece on our person, so we looked for the sun. It was getting lower in the western sky. We knew we had about three hours of daylight left. Time to pack up and head for the barn (a phrase often used by my father; it means to head towards home or go to bed).

We rode south towards home. We passed the men working on the tree stump. They appeared tired and looked at us longingly as if wishing it were, they out for a day of fun.

We said our goodnights and briefly discussed going out again soon. We all agreed it was enjoyable. Someone suggested the following week, and in unison, we all said yes.

I had managed not to think about Belle or the onyx figurine for some time. I was busy with my social life. It seems these days that is about all I must think about. The men are herding cattle out towards Winslow. Their trip's home seems to be a spur-of-the-moment trip. Nellie is living in Yucca, and Tillie is busy being a homemaker.

The planned outing with the girls came around fast. We discussed going in a different direction. I guess we are creatures of habit and chose to go North again.

As we rode our horses past the men digging the stump, we were rather shocked to see that it appeared not much progress had been made. There were more men this time, and several were standing around, scratching their beards and rubbing their heads. It appears they were busy trying to figure out how to go about getting the remainder of the tree out of the ground.

We thought we had made it by this time without catcalls. As we passed by, the same man whistled. This time we did not giggle. One of the girls waved an indiscreet gesture with her hand. We did not want to appear rude and un-neighborly, nor did we wish to encourage their behavior. Most men will stop once they realize that the woman is not accepting of his actions.

Marie said she felt uncomfortable knowing the men were a short distance away from us and suggested that we ride further north. I knew that we could head west and take the old wagon road that led over the hill. I often go that way when I am visiting Tillie. It takes you right down to the Cienega near the farm.

We rode longer than usual, so this cut our lunchtime shorter. We rode home, avoiding the area that the men were working.

Several weeks had passed since we had taken our journey in the direction of the men. I think we were all very curious to see the progress being made on the land. We decided unanimously to head in that direction.

As we neared the property, we could see the big timber wagon with several horses tied to one end. There were plenty of men, and a few women gathered to watch as the big horses pulled on the stump. When the horses stopped, the men would grab shovels and picks and begin digging around the stump. Marie's brother happened to be one of the men working.

"Hello, Ernest." Yelled Marie, very excited to see him.

He motioned for us to come over his way. Hesitantly, the other girls and I made our way over to him.

She explained how we had watched over the last several weeks the tedious process of removing the large monstrosity.

He told us that John, [the man building the house], worked with him as a lumberman. John convinced the owner of the mill to bring the big wagon and horses to help.

Suddenly, I realized that the group of women had moved closer to us. A young woman waved to me. She had a scarf tied around her head, and I did not recognize her. As she came closer to me, I realized it was Belle. Excitedly, I went towards her. We began conversing with each other, and I quickly learned that this was to be her cabin. She and John married at the beginning of summer. She appeared to be very excited about the prospect of a home of her own and family. She pointed him out to me, and I gasped as I realized he was the man who had been doing the catcalls. Immediately, I started to say something to her but decided against it for fear of possibly hurting her feelings.

As timing would have it, the stump made a cracking sound as it let loose of its eternal grip on the earth. It was as if the tree let out a grieving moan of defeat as the stump inched its way along the ground. Mother Nature sent a powerful surge of wind at that very moment, creating a cloud of dust to shower over everyone standing near. We had all just witnessed her anger at humanity. A ponderosa pine tree is scared and worshiped as being an astute and formidable creation of a higher power.

I could truly feel Mother Nature's disgust with man today.

Belle looked over at me with obviously the same feeling that I had experienced. I thought for a moment that she was going to cry. Then we were suddenly brought back to reality by a loud cheer from everyone watching. Were we the only ones paying attention to this eternal being?

When the moment allowed, I asked her if she had felt the sadness coming from the earth. She responded with the shaking of her head in agreement. She said that only people who have a gift of listening to the world around them could hear such things. Most humans choose to ignore what the earth is saying to us.

"That is why I knew I could tell you the premonition I had about you so long ago. I knew you would someday grow to understand its meaning." Belle said. "You did not laugh at me and call me names like the girls at school did."

"No, thank you for warning me of the dangers I face. I do not understand it and wish to know more of this threat of the black horse and the man I love."

"Maybe one day we can meet, and I can use my Ouija board to discover more. I only have limited knowledge of my visions. I cannot see everything in one's future. You may desire not to know everything, as it would alter the way you live your life. Some feel that if humans are given too many facts, it would be harmful. Think long and hard about it before you approach me for a reading. You cannot erase it from your mind once you are told. For that, I apologize for telling you when we were so young. I did not yet learn the full force of my powers, nor the control of my excitement. Please forgive me, my friend. I wish you only good and happiness."

"You are forgiven, and although the black horse has kept reappearing in my life, I chose long ago not to dwell on its negative side. I will heed the warning but not dwell on becoming pessimistic. You are a good friend, and I wish you happiness."

We went off on our weekly adventure as we had planned. Someone asked me why I was so solitary today. I chose not to explain and blamed it on a girl's time of the month. That led everyone to discuss the distress of our curse.

As the weeks went by, we watched the cabin being constructed and endured the man's perseverance in trying to get our attention. My heart ached each time for Belle. I prayed that John would be faithful to her, knowing that he would probably wind up being a charlatan. I knew that even if someone tried to warn her, she would not heed their advice. Besides, she has probably already seen the future and decided not to dwell on the future. Just like me.

Dear LJ,

I have had quite the adventure lately with my girlfriends. I am learning that we must create our own destiny in life. Living is not easy and often very difficult. We share it with everyone, even though some preferred not to accept the reality of life. That too, I am learning is acceptable. As a wise man once said, "To each his own choices."

Choose wisely when you confront Mother Nature, as she is a powerful being, and you are but one of her children.

CHAPTER 31

Never Again Ed~I Swear It.

Flagstaff, Arizona Territory~1893
Age~17

I felt like being alone as I walked south down towards Milltown. It was a beautiful early fall day. There was a light breeze, which in Flagstaff was rare that it was light and not a strong wind. Wind at 7,000 feet was just part of the climate. Therefore, I was appreciative of a light breeze. The days were still very warm, but there was a feeling of fall. Hard to describe, I thought to myself that just yesterday, it had been summer, and today there was a slight change. I could sense it. Wrapped up in thought, I did not notice that someone was walking behind me. A slight pull on my hat bow startled me and brought me out of my daydream.

"Hey, beautiful," Ed said as I turned around. "Where are you off to this gorgeous morning?"

"Walking, silly, can't you tell?" I said, teasingly. I began noticing my heart feeling as if it were in my stomach. Could he hear it pounding with excitement? I wondered? I did not see or hear from him in months. I was busy with my job and my own social life.

"Want a friend, or do you want to be alone," Ed questioned, not wanting to intrude on my walk. He understood that when you needed to be by yourself, there was nothing to be done except being alone. Cowboys are loners. They can go for weeks without seeing or talking to anyone.

"Walk with me," I demanded.

"I was looking for you, saw your family downtown, and you weren't with them," Ed said inquisitively.

"Yeah, I had enough of the family for one day. I thought I might walk down to the cemetery and visit mama's grave." I said quietly. It was nice to have mama buried in Flagstaff instead of Albuquerque like my father. He was too far away.

Suddenly, a pack of dogs was running toward us. Ed was ready to grab his gun to scare them away when I jumped into his arms. He wanted to lecture me about my action, but the dogs were closing in on us. He shot towards them but did not harm them. The dog packs in town were becoming a real problem for people.

I held on tightly to his neck as the dogs ran off. Ed found himself enjoying me in his arms. My breasts rubbed against his chest. My cheeks turned red in embarrassment. I was glad he did not see my face.

Excitedly, he asked me to be his date for the Military Ball next month.

"Oh good," I said, talking aloud. "I already have a date for the dance on Saturday night at Hawk's Hall. However, I will attend the Military ball with you." I said curtly. I did not want him to know that I lusted over him and would prefer to go with him instead of Bill Shroyer.

"There is a dance on Saturday?" Ed asked disappointingly. "Who is the lucky guy?"

I said that it was Bill Shroyer.

"You mean that man who was a friend of your mama's and claims to be a gold miner and is twice your age?" Retorted Ed with an ample amount of jealousy in his voice.

I did not have a reply for that. Ed had never once shown any jealousy. Is he really jealous? I was on cloud nine as we walked down towards the cemetery. Ed left me alone to sit by my mother's grave. I wanted so much for her to be there right now so that I could ask her for advice on men. Married sisters don't offer much help. Especially since both are expecting babies soon.

Nellie's advice is always "Mind your p's and q's." I returned a snide remark to her, stating that 'p is for proper and q is for questionable."

Bill asked me first, and I would honor that, but if Ed just happened to be at the dance and asked me…. I would have to be polite and dance with him, too. Problem solved.

"Ed, I have an idea," I shouted excitedly. "If you show up and ask me to dance, I will have to dance with you."

"Will you pick up my body when Mr. Shroyer belts me in the mouth?" He laughed, appreciating my idea. "Or better yet, kiss me?" He joked as he picked me up and threw me over his shoulder.

I was pounding him on his back, acting as if I was protesting, but loving every moment of his undivided attention. Because Ed was a friend of my entire family, it was very seldom I was ever alone with the man. Suddenly, he pulled me forward and began kissing me on the lips. I could feel his tongue sliding between my lips, and I gasped.

"Why, Miss Liz Hoffman, is this your first kiss from a man?" he said as he kissed me again.

My mind was racing, and my heart pounding. I started to answer when he stopped me from saying anything. I did not want this moment to end. I had always loved him, but I never knew that he felt the same.

The sun was getting lower in the sky when we realized we should begin walking back to town. I realized that my family would be getting worried since I had been gone all day. However, when Ed asked me to go to dinner with him, I did not hesitate.

We entered the restaurant together as people turned to stare. He was a tall, dark shaggy-haired man who had not had a haircut in weeks, and I was a petite pretty girl. Gasps could be heard when they realized that it was me with the man. I greeted people I knew with an air of importance.

Secrets in this town were in the paper the next day, anyway, so why not make the most of it. Gossip, they could. I could not be prouder. The town tomboy had a man on my arm.

Halfway through a huge steak that Ed had ordered for me, I almost choked as Bert and George walked inside the restaurant. They had been searching for me for close to two hours. While they were looking for me, they ran into someone who had just left the restaurant and told them where I was. There was anger in their faces.

I never liked to see my brothers get mad at me. Usually, I would have tears come to my eyes, and that would stop them in their tracks. I had to remind myself, not this time. I was a woman now; Ed told me so himself. I would defend myself. I did not show Ed; I was a baby.

However, Ed had other ideas. Not wanting to insult my brothers, he insisted that he had been nothing but chivalrous towards their sister. He told them that the two of us had walked and that we were both hungry when we reached downtown.

George requested that Ed was to ask next time for permission when he took his sister on a walk.

I, humiliated by the talk between my brothers and Ed, sat and fumed. The men did not even acknowledge that I was sitting there. How could he have kissed me one-minute and then acted as if I were not even present the next?

Without the men noticing, I quietly removed myself from the restaurant.

Ed Geddes would have to bow down to me and beg me forgiveness before I would kiss that man again.

Arriving home, I told my family that I was sorry for making them worry and hurried off to bed. The family concluded, after a long talk, that I was a woman. The tomboy whom they all knew and loved was now all grown-up.

George, Bertie, and Ed did not understand why I would be upset. Three confirmed bachelors trying to figure a woman out made me laugh.

Tragedy struck us again when we least suspected it. Nellie gave birth to a baby boy, Emmett, who was born with a hole at the bottom of his spine. She was told he had spina-bifida. He would need constant care. If anyone could do that, it was Nellie. The doctor warned her not to get too attached to the baby, as he would not live a long life. You can never tell Nellie not to get too attached to a baby. She would take her chances and give him all the love and care he deserves.

Nellie was living with her family in a tiny railroad town named Yucca. She would need help with the three children: George, Nell, and Emmett. I reluctantly moved to Yucca to help my sister with her children. It would certainly get me away from the men in my life. A break I must have been looking for.

This would be a new adventure for me…Nurse-maid Lizzie.

Dear LJ,

Are you ready to move to Yucca? It is hot, and the wind blows hotter than hell itself. There is no way to cool yourself down. Wait until I tell Lettie. Just think she offered me a chance to stay in Chicago with her last year. She said I should become a doctor right along with her.

A way out of your problems isn't always the right way. We eventually must face them.

CHAPTER 32

Final Rejection-Maybe

Flagstaff And Williams, Arizona
Territory~March 1895
Age~18

I love to sit and listen to Bill Shroyer tell his stories of Colorado and his search for gold. He had done well mining, or so he said, just too many people moving in. Same with Flagstaff, time to get away from civilization. He is considering going to South Africa. The gold strike was prolific.

I am evaluating my relationships. Bill is an older man, although not much older than Ed. It is not uncommon for a younger woman to marry an older man. Bill is a very polite, even-tempered man. Not like Ed, who flies off the handle at every little thing. Bill is predictable, where Ed is not.

The relationship with Bill is making a change towards something more serious. I think that it is time to tell Ed just how much I love him before committing any further with Bill.

Ed comes first in my heart.

I woke up excited; an idea had come to me the day before. I always kept up with the happenings of the world by reading the local newspaper. This time, the newspaper advertised a dance in William's. I have attended dances before in William's, but not by myself. I want to surprise Ed; my mind immediately started concocting preparations. I have never been so bold and forward with Ed. The thought is intoxicating to me. The time has come for me to express my love for him. I have been extremely patient, waiting for him to make a move, I thought to myself. Tonight, I will do the forbidden task of professing my love and intention of marrying him. I, being in his town of William's, will make it easier on him. There will be none of my friends to sidetrack us.

A strong March wind caught me off guard as I stepped from the train that evening in William's. The conductor grabbed my arm just before I fell to the ground. Gathering my senses, I wondered if this was a warning to turn around and go back to Flagstaff. I quickly shrugged off my insecurities and proceeded down the street to the dance hall.

I arrived early to the dance. Luckily, I am not the only one who arrived before the scheduled time. People come from all over for a good time. I can be friendly and enjoy visiting with people while we wait for the dance to begin.

The band arrived very early, having already set up their instruments.

I spotted my friend, Jenny, from Winslow, sitting with a group of young people enjoying sandwiches made by the local women.

"Lizzie, I am so happy to see you. I was afraid I wouldn't know anyone here tonight." As Jenny's layers of petticoats bounced up and down as she crossed the room hurriedly.

"I'm happy to see you, too!" I said, not knowing if I was pleased or if I lose my confidence with friends around. "Where is the punch? I need a drink."

"The punch always starts out weak. You know that, don't you?" Jenny said, laughing. "They know that the men add to it as the evening goes along."

"Thanks for telling me. I'll make sure I drink plenty." I said as I gulped down the first cup, followed by one after another.

I was feeling quite giddy as the locals began arriving. The town band began to play, and the dance floor began to fill with gaiety.

I refused dance proposals, not wanting to take my eyes off the front door to watch for Ed to arrive. An hour into the dance, Ed still did not make an appearance. My apprehension began to grow; my mind began to race. I began to wonder whether he will even appear.

Jenny asked me if I was alright. "You are not yourself tonight. I haven't seen you dance at all, and that is unusual."

"I am just waiting for someone to show up."

"You playing the wallflower won't make him show up any sooner."

Just then, a very nice-looking, well-dressed man asked me to dance. After taking another sip of punch, I agreed to dance with him.

The man began by making small talk as we danced around the room. The punch is beginning to make me feel lightheaded. I am not used to drinking that amount of alcohol at once. I excused myself to find the lavatory.

As fate would have it, Ed entered the dance hall while I was indisposed. He had with him a tall blonde headed, scantily dressed, older woman attached to him. Ed's intoxication was obvious to everyone present as he said in a very loud voice, "I need a stiff drink, don't you sweetie pie?"

"Whatever you say, honey," The blonde-haired woman said, practically slobbering all over him as she kissed him.

At that moment, I reentered the dance hall and immediately went from feeling like a lovely woman to a silly child.

Ed looked up from the kiss, directed a scowling glare right at me. He then returned to kissing the blonde-haired woman.

The blonde-headed, blue-eyed bitch scowled at me. I immediately noticed her wrinkled face. The woman reminded me of the pictures of the ugly witches that I had seen in a book. She did not take her eyes off me. A chill ran down the back of my spine as if the woman were trying to place a spell on me.

I ran out the door and down the street without stopping to look back. I could hear someone running behind me. Is it the old witch? Run…

I was running as fast as I could in a long dress with layers of petticoats. "Damn things!" I mumbled to myself. I could not see in the dark. I could not see the mud hole that was directly in front of me. I felt my shoe; it was stuck in the mud. As I reached down to retrieve my shoe and foot, I felt a familiar large hand on my shoulder. Ed had come after me. He started to apologize when suddenly he drew me in close to his body, leaned over, and placed his lips right on top of me, forcing my mouth open. I was helpless and seemed to melt in his arms. My senses came rushing back to me, and I abruptly slapped him directly across the cheek as he started to speak. I alarmed him, to put it nicely.

"Damn you, Liz," he said, rubbing the side of his face, "why did you go and ruin a good kiss."

"Go kiss your whore. I have better things to do with my life than wait for you to grow up," I said angrily.

"Me? You are saying I am not a grown man. That is hilarious, Cyclone. Now, you just simmer down, or I will have to kiss you again," he teased.

"Not me, I am not your whore," I whispered, trying not to attract very much attention. Then I realized that it was too late. A crowd gathered around us from the dance.

"I am too old to change, baby. Do you know how long I have waited for you to grow up? I have waited for years and years! I am not one to sit back and wait for anybody. Heck Liz, you know I spend my life on the back of a horse and in a saloon. What kind of life will that be for you?" He tried explaining.

"Eddie, baby, are you gonna be all night talking to that little girl?" squealed the blond-haired vixen. "Take me to your place."

"Go home Liz, and I promise I'll come to see you. We can talk, just you and me. I won't even take a drink that day, and I won't have a gun on me, honest," he said while walking towards the blonde-haired woman.

I turned without saying a word and began walking toward the train station. Alone, rejected, and tipsy. My head was spinning. I did not like this feeling of no control.

Suddenly, I felt someone following me. I slowed my walk down, thinking that it was Jenny.

As I turned around to look, he grabbed me from behind, causing my shoes to fall off. He kissed me hard and long. Distraught, I planted a firm fist in his eye.

Without so much as a word between us, I turned, picked my shoes out of the mud, and walked down the street, not even turning to look back. How dare he, he kissed me after rejecting me in front of that slut. Who does he think he is?

I seated myself on the bench inside the train station. Uncontrollable tears streamed down my face.

A man, seeing me cry, offered me his handkerchief. I quickly obliged, thanking him in between sobs.

Suddenly without warning, Ed appeared in the train station. "Don't you ever, and I mean you will never do that to me again, do you understand? Sometimes you act just like a child."

The blonde woman, attached to his arm, turned and gave me a sneer.

Ed turned and left the train station without another word, leaving me alone in my sorrow. I boarded the next train to Flagstaff, swearing revenge to Ed. I will show him what a real woman is and that I did not need him insulting me in public. I was leaving behind the only man who ever made the butterflies swarm inside my belly. I love him with all my heart and soul; I always have and always will.

I stood at the back of the caboose, shoeless, mud up to my knees. The mud on my face washed off only by the tears running down my cheeks. I stood watching him fade out of my life. Well, this time, anyway.

The next day, I went to see Tillie. Lucky for me, the baby was sleeping. Her life was exactly as she had planned it out. Husband and baby with her on a farm.

I was happy for her. She and Jesse were a good match. We talked for a while, and I told her about the night before. I confessed to her that I thought the only way for me to end the fiasco of a relationship is for me to leave the territory.

"Bill tells Jesse all the time how much he cares for you. Would you consider him?"

"Anything is better than a man who is a drinker, a fighter, and carries a gun. He gets so angry he scares me."

"You would be wise to avoid him for a while. I know how hard it is for you. You have always loved him."

It was good to talk to my sister. If I can just gather the strength, I need to tell him to get out of my life. Easier said than done.

I was so wrapped up in Ed that I did not see what I was doing to Bill.

I went looking for him, only to find out he had gone to the hills around Prescott to mine.

I am alone, but that is good. I will have time for me. I am not sad or angry with Ed. He is a cowboy; they are loners; they work hard, play harder, and love many. Maybe one day, he will settle down with me.

Dear LJ,

I could not believe the man had the nerve to kiss me after showing up with some other woman at the dance. You would have been so proud of me.

He cannot come around to my house when he is drunk, angry, and carries a gun. Those three things mixed together make a volatile situation. Anything can happen, and it won't be good.

When you chase after your dream, pray that it does not turn into a nightmare.

The End…well, maybe.

Author's Afterthoughts

I hope you enjoyed reading "You Can Call Me Lizzie," as much as I enjoyed writing it.

I think about her life and how exciting it was to be on the cusp of change. The turn of the century offered people new opportunities to travel and explore the world.

Imagine people getting on a train in Flagstaff and traveling to the East is amazing.

They were at the beginning of a change in this country. Their curiosity for the world around them was sparked

They were not alienated in the world around them. It was a glorious time to be alive. However, you had to be brave.

Women's Right to Vote and the Temperance movement were moving ahead. They knew the time was right to pursue those rights.

It took women like Lizzie to brave the world and show men that women can do what men can.

She was one of many who wanted a different life for themselves. It is because of women like her that we women today have opportunities. It is up to us to persevere and press forward not to give up on those demands and rights. If she had accepted life for what it was and said, "Oh well," where would we be.

Life back then was not easy. Tragedies were a common occurrence. It is what made them strong. They were survivors.

Thank you for sharing with me the life of this strong and courageous woman.

Remember, if you find yourself thinking about her or get goosebumps, then you my friend,

"Have been bitten by the Lizzie bug."

Congratulations!

Books by JK Hoffman

"Forgotten Cowgirl, A woman of Character in the Arizona Territory." Formerly known as "Flagstaff's Forgotten Cowgirl, The Journals of Lizzie Hoffman."

Coming Soon,
Curse of the Tiburon